FIENDS WITH BENEFITS

A PARANORMAL MYSTERY ADVENTURE

MONSTERS OF JELLYFISH BEACH 2

WARD PARKER

MAD MANGROVE MEDIA, LLC

CONTENTS

CHAPTER 1
BEWARE OF DATING APPS

"I thought all vampires were sexy. Boy, was I wrong. I mean, he has *liver spots*! I didn't know vampires could get those."

The woman was in her early thirties, old enough to know better. Her hair was black and cut short. She wore a business-casual outfit of a white sleeveless blouse, black pants, and high heels. The impression she gave was of confident intelligence. Not the kind of woman who would be deluded by Hollywood fantasies of vampires.

What bothered me most was the fact that she was dating an actual vampire. Humans weren't supposed to know vampires existed.

"Courtney, why have you come to us?" asked my business partner Luisa, a *santera*, or Santeria priestess.

The three of us sat in the back room of the Jellyfish Beach Mystical Mart and Botanica. It was 8:30 p.m., and we had closed for the night.

"A friend of mine told me about your store and that you and Missy truly know about supernatural stuff. That you didn't just sell bogus trinkets to superstitious old ladies."

Luisa's expression darkened, but I rolled with the insult. I had once believed the same thing about botanicas. As I became more advanced in witchcraft, and needed certain ingredients for my spells and potions I couldn't find online, I became a fan of botanicas.

"Yes, we know a lot about the supernatural," Luisa said. Her Cuban accent came on more powerfully when she was annoyed. "What exactly do you need?"

"I want you to break the vampire's hold over me. He turned out to be much older than I expected. In the dating app, he said he was old—three hundred years old. All that means is he was turned into a vampire three hundred years ago. I figured, so what? It only means he's wiser and more sophisticated. He posted photos of a guy in his forties. Definitely good-looking. But when we met, the truth came out. He's really in his late sixties. That's the age he was when he was turned."

"I'm sure that happens all the time with dating apps," I said.

"Yes, but the guys who mislead you about their age aren't vampires who can mesmerize you."

"Wait, how did he get a photo of himself in his forties if he was turned three hundred years ago?" Luisa asked. "They didn't have cameras when he was in his forties."

"It's a stock photo he grabbed online. Some guy who looks kind of like him."

"He mesmerized you into dating him?" Luisa asked with

skepticism. "I thought they had the power to lure victims into being fed upon and then to forget about it afterward."

"It's more than that. He has a hold over me. I'm completely powerless with him. Every time he wants to get together, I agree, even though I don't want to. Every time I try to break up with him, he changes my mind."

"It sounds to me like your typical unhealthy relationship," Luisa said.

"Not to get too personal, but does he feed on you?" I asked. "Or do you simply . . . date?"

"He fed lightly on me a few times at the beginning, but I let him know it freaked me out. Now, we're only romantic together. Though I don't love him."

"What makes you think we can break his hold over you?" I asked.

"You're the only people I know of who have supernatural expertise. I'm desperate and don't know what to do."

I knew vampires and how manipulative they could be, though I've never been in a relationship with one. I didn't count my ex-husband, who had been turned while he was cheating on me.

"I know some spells that could help you get out of a relationship," I said, "but I don't know if they work on vampires."

"Do you know any vampires?" Courtney asked.

"I know several. Seniors like your boyfriend."

She cringed when I said boyfriend. I didn't mention that I've had extensive dealings with vampires. Until recently, I had been working full time as a home-health nurse at retirement communities for vampires, werewolves, and other supernatural creatures.

"What's your, um, friend's name, and where does he live?"

"Hugh Humbert. He lives in Squid Tower at the beach. They're all old vampires there."

I was quite familiar with Squid Tower, because many of those old vampires had been my patients. To passersby, it looked like a typical retirement community with shuffleboard and pickleball courts. Except that no residents were ever outside in the daytime.

"Can you guys help me?" Courtney asked.

What she didn't realize was that Luisa and I had only recently begun taking on cases involving the supernatural. We now went beyond simply selling products and performing Santeria and voodoo ceremonies. We cataloged and monitored all the supernatural and mythological creatures in the area.

However, aside from recently exonerating a ghoul who was accused of murdering a human, our expertise in being supernatural fixers was limited. We'd certainly never dealt with a problem vampire before. But I was willing to try.

"How do you imagine we'd get him to leave you alone?" I asked. "Give him a potion to make him fall out of love with you?"

"He doesn't love me. It's all physical with him."

"I have a charm that protects women from men," Luisa said. "Don't know if it would work on a vampire."

Courtney shook her head no.

Luisa and I couldn't threaten Humbert with physical harm. We weren't thugs. All we had were magic and spells, and we didn't practice the kind that hurt people.

I did, however, possess nursing skills. Old people have ailments, and vampires are no exception, despite their supernatural wound-healing abilities. But sickness is another matter. If Humbert had an ailment and I promised to cure it, he might be willing to meet me. And during my consultation, I could gently convince him to release his hold over Courtney in exchange for treating his ailment.

I asked her if he had any nagging health concerns.

"Some minor ones, like arthritis in his knees," Courtney said. "After all, he was turned in his late sixties. There's one that bothers him most." She giggled. "Type O intolerance."

"What?" In all my years of being a home-health nurse for vampires, I'd never had a patient with this condition.

"Just like some humans have an intolerance for dairy, Hugh can't feed on someone with Type O blood without serious intestinal distress. It's bad enough to ruin an entire evening, he says. He would be so grateful to get rid of that."

"Do you have Type O?" Luisa asked.

Courtney shook her head. "AB negative."

"Too bad. If you had Type O, you might not need our help."

"I told you he doesn't feed on me anymore. He has other interests."

"There's a blood bus that brings meals to Squid Tower for the residents who can't or won't hunt," I said. "He only needs to let them know his dietary restrictions."

"Yeah, I've seen the bus. It drives into the parking lot like an ice-cream truck, playing stupid music. You should see the vampires come running. But Hugh is picky about hunting for his meals. He prefers luring women into having dates with him. And he expects his dinner guests to be friends with benefits."

"Gross!" Luisa said.

"I've got to get free of him. Please help me."

"I could attempt to find a magical cure for his Type O intolerance if he promises to leave you alone," I said.

"Magical? Are you a witch?"

"Possibly," I said with a smile.

Her face lit up with hope. "I'll tell him to call you."

"Okay," I said, a little worried that I couldn't deliver.

Luisa looked at me with narrowed eyes. She gave the impression she didn't want to take on the case, but she knew about all my vampire connections.

Courtney asked, "How much do you charge?"

I was about to give our hourly rates when Luisa interrupted me.

"We must confer with the spirits first. They will tell us, and we will tell you."

Two days later, after the *orisha* Ogún told Luisa we should charge $150 per hour, I set about doing preliminary work on the case. First, I needed to find out everything I could about Courtney's problem boyfriend.

Hugh Humbert, like all conscientious vampires, had few searchable records online. The only exceptions were his dating app profile and the county property appraiser's listing of his condo. I assumed he had an account on the Fangbook social-media site, but that was just for vampires, and outsiders like me couldn't access it.

I called Agnes, the president of the Squid Tower HOA and the community's nest mother. She knew little about Humbert, except that he was semi-retired from the financial services industry. Beatrice, the community busybody, would know more, she told me.

"Missy? Good to hear from you," said Beatrice Costa, a former patient. "I miss seeing you. Have you completely retired from healthcare?"

"I still care for patients from time to time, but my full-time job is running a retail establishment. I'm calling to ask if you know Hugh Humbert."

She paused before answering. "Why?" Her voice was dark and flat.

She obviously wasn't a fan. "I have a client who hired me to resolve a dispute between them."

"No one resolves disputes with Humbert. He always makes his victims go away empty-handed."

"Victims? Of what?"

"Hugh Humbert is a money manager. He's known for making clients fantastically rich so they can spend eternity in luxury. But he's also lost millions for other clients on dubious investments. Half the vampires who know him say he's a genius. The other half say he's a crook."

"Which half are you?"

"He's a crook. But my opinion is based on what I've heard. My husband and I never invested with him."

Since she wasn't a fan of his, I could be more honest with her. I explained my client was a human who'd been mesmerized into dating him.

"That doesn't surprise me one bit," Beatrice said. "I hope he hasn't taken all her money, too."

So did I because Luisa and I wanted to be paid.

"His clients are lucky he can't mesmerize other vampires, or he'd have even more victims. He should go after gullible humans and leave us alone."

"I think humans prefer money managers who work daytime hours," I said.

As soon as I got off the call, I researched blood diseases. Intolerance to drinking certain blood types didn't appear in any searches. Nor did ill effects from drinking blood at all. You know why?

Because humans don't drink blood, at least not regularly. It's unhealthy for us. And medical researchers don't acknowledge vampires exist.

Frankly, as a nurse, I was pretty good at drawing blood. There was no need to keep up on the latest medical journal studies on blood composition. Certainly not on any that were about drinking it.

There wasn't a cure for dairy intolerance, so why should there be one for Type O blood intolerance? There were medications, prescribed and over the counter, that could help prevent milk from sending you on endless pilgrimages to the bathroom. I doubted there were any that did the same for blood.

I would need to use magic to stop Type O's insidious effect on Hugh Humbert. Assuming I could find a spell that would work.

And assuming its efficacy would convince Humbert to release his hold on Courtney.

Was it even worth all my effort?

The memory of Courtney's haunted eyes told me yes. As did the amount on the invoice I emailed to her for a down payment.

I was leafing through my grimoires, sneezing from the dust arising from their ancient pages, when my phone rang.

"Ms. Mindle, it's Courtney Peppers. I spoke to Humbert and told him you have a cure for his blood intolerance. He's willing to meet with you."

"Awesome," I said.

Now, all I needed to do was find the cure.

CHAPTER 2

DOUBLE, DOUBLE TOIL AND TUMMY TROUBLE

I t's been several years since I evolved from hobbyist witch to semi-pro. I say semi-pro because few witches can make a professional living with the craft. My biological mother could, as a black-magic-sorceress-for-hire. It was a paltry income, and she sold her soul so long ago, she's forgotten what the words morality and integrity mean.

Practitioners of white magic like me don't summon demons. Ordering demons to assassinate people is where the good money is, if you can sell your services to the various dictators, strongmen, and evil CEOs of the world. We benevolent witches must be content with making a few bucks here and there with love potions and beauty spells. That's why I have a day job.

Dealing in healing spells was tricky. As a nurse, I had a keen interest in them, but I hadn't felt right billing for my spells, aside from the cost of any ingredients and what my home-health agency charged. The powers I drew upon from within and from the earth didn't feel like things I should charge for. They felt like gifts to me, to be passed on to the ill and injured.

So, here I was, trying to develop a spell to cure a blood-type intolerance, the cost of which would be buried in the "consultant" fees Luisa and I were charging. If this were a medical cure for a human disease, the pharmaceutical or bioengineering companies could make billions off it. Here, in my little world of magic, I was practically doing it for free to convince a vampire to give up his human girlfriend.

Unlike a Big Pharma scientist, I was going about it randomly and intuitively, perusing centuries-old grimoires, diaries written by American folk healers, and a book about the remedies of the indigenous people of Florida.

No one had written a spell to heal Type O blood intolerance in vampires.

"Don Mateo, I need your help!" I called out.

Don Mateo was my assistant, in a fashion. He was the ghost of a sorcerer from the 1600s who had come to America fleeing the Spanish Inquisition. After a spell intended to entertain a friend went wrong, and he was eaten by a demon, he left behind a copy of the grimoire *The Key of Solomon*. The back pages of the volume were filled with his hand-written spells, influenced by native Timucuan shamans. When I inherited the spell book from my father, Don Mateo's ghost came with it.

"Don Mateo, I need your assistance with a healing spell."

A thump and a crash came from my bedroom. Yes, Don Mateo had materialized in my underwear drawer again. That old pervert.

A one-piece bathing suit that no longer fit floated into the living room. It hovered in front of where I sat on the couch and appeared to be inflating. Now it looked as if it were being worn by an invisible person with entirely the wrong physique. Namely, a chubby man.

A painful groan and a curse in archaic Spanish filled the air. Finally, the bathing suit dropped to the ground and Don Mateo materialized, wearing breeches and a waistcoat.

"At your service, madam," he said, bowing and sweeping his spectral wide-brimmed hat before him.

"I won't even ask what you were doing with my swimsuit," I said.

"Thank you."

"Well, my phantasmal friend, do you know anything about healing vampires?"

His apparition was fully visible, enough so I could read the expression of surprise on his face.

"No, madam. I have always tried to avoid vampires, especially since the Inquisition was rumored to have many among its ranks."

"Did the Native Americans have vampires?"

"Not like the European version. The Timucua had other demonic creatures in their folklore. I heard the tales, but fortunately, never encountered one of these creatures."

"Did you hear of any spells concerning them?"

"Only spells to keep them away. Not for healing them. Are you asking because you still have patients at Squid Tower?"

"I still see a few patients there, but this is not for them. It's for a vampire with an intolerance for Type O blood. Or maybe it's an allergy. In any event, I'm going to offer him a cure in exchange for releasing his hold on a mortal woman."

"What is Type O blood?"

"Blood types were discovered long after you departed the world of the living. I won't go into details, but all blood is not the same. If you're having a blood transfusion, you need to receive the same type as yours."

"What if you are being bled by leeches?"

"Never mind. It's odd, though, that he would be intolerant or allergic to only one blood type. But he wouldn't survive if it was for all types, I guess. Do you know any spells for intestinal problems?"

"I know many. Back in my day, we didn't have boxes like that." He pointed toward the kitchen refrigerator. "Stomach and intestinal problems were quite common, and I know some handy spells for them. But have you considered another possibility?"

"What?"

"That this vampire is not suffering a biological disorder. What if he has been hexed?"

"You mean someone put a curse on him?"

"Exactly. Perhaps whoever hexed him wanted to prevent him from drinking all blood types so he would starve. Instead, it only worked for Type O."

"Or it is the blood type of the witch who hexed him, and the witch didn't want to be a meal anymore."

"Good thinking," Don Mateo said.

I shook my head in frustration. "I just want to convince him to leave my client alone. Teach me your most powerful spell for digestive problems. I'll have to work with that."

"I shall, but I will need some special ingredients."

"Like what?"

"I will need a pair of your silk panties."

"Don Mateo, knock it off, you weirdo!"

He blushed. Yes, I actually made a ghost blush.

⊶⋔⋔⋔⋔⋔⊷

CONJURING the spell wasn't all that difficult for me, but I needed to write down the Latin words of the incantation. To test the spell, I accepted an invitation from my friend, Matt, for a home-cooked meal. His chili never failed to put me in distress a couple of hours after eating it. Fortunately, I was already home when the discomfort began and immediately cast the spell.

It worked magnificently. Yes, it was only a temporary remedy, but I could enchant an amulet with the spell. Humbert could carry the amulet with him when feeding, like a roll of antacid tablets.

"I'm hurt, I tell ya, like I've been slapped in the face."

The New York accent made me turn my head to find a four-foot-long green iguana staring at me from atop my washing machine. It was Tony, the iguana who was supposed to serve as my witch's familiar. The Friends of Cryptids Society gave him to me, and I haven't quite gotten used to him yet.

"What's wrong?" I asked.

"You need a spell, and the first guy you ask for help is that silly wizard's ghost?"

"He knew a lot of spells as a wizard, and I have his grimoire."

"Spare me. He was a failed wizard. He died from his own magic."

"Technically, a demon killed him."

"A demon he summoned by mistake."

"You two were friends," I reminded Tony.

"Yeah. So what? I'm your witch's familiar. He isn't."

"Are you jealous?"

"Iguanas don't get jealous. We get ticked off."

The crest on his head was standing fully upright. I guess that was a warning sign.

"A generic spell to relieve indigestion ain't gonna help with a blood-type intolerance."

Tony knew what I was up to because he was telepathic. That was supposed to be a benefit, but I found it to be more of an annoyance.

"The intolerance comes from the inability to digest," Tony mansplained. "People with lactose intolerance don't have enough of the enzyme lactase. And all humans lack the enzymes and microorganisms needed to digest whole blood. Creatures like vampire bats and vampires have them."

"I don't need a lecture from an iguana."

"Sorry, Missy, but you do. Your spell's gotta mimic the enzymes and microorganisms needed for digesting blood and all its iron. I admit I don't know why Type O is so sketchy."

"Okay, Mister Smarty-pants. How will my spell do that?"

"Use a creature that feeds on blood. Get some fleas from your stupid cats."

"My cats are not stupid, and they do not have fleas."

"Whatever. So go outside tonight and slap a few mosquitoes. And get a sample of Type O from a human."

I have Type A, but I knew that Matt had Type O. No, it's not weird that I know his blood type. I'm a nurse, remember? Grabbing my blood-work kit, I drove straight to his bungalow, which still reeked of his chili.

"I need a sample of your blood," I announced.

"I have never been so used by a woman before," he said with a smile, not at all surprised by my request.

After I took a single tube of his blood, I returned home and collected several mosquitoes that I slapped before they drank any of my own blood. Then, I mixed the insects in a small bowl with yarrow, mandrake, and other ingredients I don't care to divulge. Matt's blood was added last.

Even though Tony should have been sleeping at this hour, his voice telepathically popped into my head, offering suggestions as I custom-built a spell to activate the magical recipe. It went into an amulet.

Like my previous spell, this would not permanently cure Humbert's Type O intolerance. Unlike the previous spell, this one would allow him to digest the blood.

Mission accomplished. Thanks to a freaking iguana.

I called Courtney, and she promised to get word to Humbert that a spell to treat his peculiar stomach ailment was ready. She would give him my number and email address, she promised me.

Nights went by with no word from the vampire. There was nothing I could do but wait for him to invite me for a visit.

I did not expect my doorbell to ring at one in the morning.

CHAPTER 3
HE'S MESMERIZING

I knew it was Humbert before he even introduced himself. It wasn't surprising that Courtney was disappointed when she met him; he was easily two decades in body age older than his profile photo of a dark-haired rakish man in his early forties. In fact, old age had begun ravaging him before he was turned, when the aging process abruptly halted.

The face that once might have been attractive now had many wrinkles. His nose was a bit too large, as were his ears. He looked like a grandpa, not a Don Juan.

"I'm Hugh Humbert, and I was referred to you by Courtney Peppers." His voice was low and velvety. He offered his hand.

"Good to meet you," I said, without shaking his hand. One must be careful when first meeting a vampire before you know if they have malevolent intent. You don't want to give them any extra advantages in manipulating you.

"Please come in." I smiled with every bit of dazzle I had in me to compensate for my snub of his hand. "Have a seat in the living room. Can I offer you wine, water, tea?" As a human, I wouldn't be expected to keep blood in my refrigerator. Even the humans who role-played being vampires couldn't stomach whole blood.

"Nothing for me, thank you." Vampires will drink liquids other than blood, but in much lower amounts than we living mortals.

"Please excuse me for a moment." I pointed to my wrinkled T-shirt and running shorts, in which I had been sleeping.

In my bedroom, I pulled on jeans and a jersey. More important, I put on an extra vampire-repellant amulet to reinforce the one I've always worn, ever since I first began working with vampires.

When I returned to the living room, Humbert was still standing. I sat on the sofa, and he eased himself into an armchair. Yes, he exhibited a hint of arthritis in his knees.

"Tell me about this cure you have for my stomach problems," he said.

"It's not a cure, but it will help you. It requires me to cast a spell upon you, and you'll need to wear an amulet when feeding. You shouldn't have problems with any blood after that."

He narrowed his eyes as he assessed me. His nostrils flared slightly. He was reading my scent for signals of deceit.

"How much will it cost me?"

"I have an interesting proposition for you," I said. "Would you be willing to barter for the treatment?"

"Barter? What do you want?"

"Courtney is my friend. I want you to free her from the hold you have over her. To break up with her, essentially."

He barked out a laugh. It was harsh and feral, startling me.

18

"How could my relationship with her be any business of yours?"

"She's a good friend." I didn't want to use the word client. "I'm concerned about her. She truly wants to break up with you, and you won't let her."

"Not true. And you make me sound like an evil fiend."

He was an evil fiend.

"Courtney is irrational," he continued, "as are so many of you ladies, vampire or human."

"I'll ignore the sexist comment, Mr. Humbert. Are you capable of understanding she feels vulnerable and sad?"

"I make her sad?"

I nodded. "She is not your property. She's an independent woman who may date whomever she pleases, or no one at all."

He shook his head. "I gave her pleasure."

"But you don't give her happiness. She has the right to be happy."

"I'm not making her do anything against her will. She's free, as far as I'm concerned."

"Mr. Humbert, I know all about mesmerizing."

His lips gave the hint of a smile. "I heard you have a lot of experience with vampires."

"I do. I've kept quite a few of them healthy. My Type O digestive treatment can be yours for free if you let Courtney go. There are plenty of other women out there for you."

"Don't I know it? I especially enjoy humans," he said, gazing at me intently. "Your sparks of life are so refreshing."

The guy had a certain charm if you overlooked the crow's feet, wrinkles, and such. The white hair was kind of attractive. As was his air of wisdom and experience.

I caught myself. What was I thinking? I had to be as cold-hearted as a prosecutor with this vampire.

"Will you accept my offer, Mr. Humbert?"

"How will you enforce it?"

"Courtney will tell me if you try to lure her back again. If so, I'll cancel the spell."

He shrugged. "You're a very clever human, aren't you?"

"I'm not clever. This is a practical arrangement. Will you accept it or not?"

"You're also very beautiful."

"Don't even think of going there," I said, standing. "We humans aren't so stupid that we don't know when we're being manipulated. Please tell me if you'll accept the offer. Otherwise, this meeting is over."

"Tell me about the spell. Is it painful?"

"Not at all." I sat down again. "We sit in a magic circle. I burn a mixture of dried herbs and other ingredients and gather energies. Then I recite the words of the incantation. It should take less than an hour. Afterward, you wear an amulet under your shirt and against your stomach. Moving forward, you won't have problems digesting any of the blood types."

"That sounds delightful," he said in a tone that was almost purring. "I can't tell if a human has Type O until I'm already drinking, and then, of course, it's too late. You can't imagine the pain and suffering. Worse than any digestive ailment I had as a human."

"It sounds horrible." I caught myself feeling sorry for him.

My right hand involuntarily touched one of the vampire-repellant amulets beneath my top, and my pity for him lessened.

Was he trying to mesmerize me? He wasn't using any tell-tale techniques, which resemble those of a hypnotist. But I guess an experienced vampire wouldn't be so obvious.

"The power for this spell comes from within you?"

"Yes. Enhanced by energy from the earth, wind, fire, water, and spirit." I didn't mention I also had a power charm that added a boost.

"Where did you get this power within you? Regular humans don't have power like that, right?"

"I was born with it," I said, touching the amulet again. "Being a witch is in my blood."

"You had it as a child?" He leaned toward me, appearing fascinated by me.

"I guess I did, but I didn't realize I had anything special until adolescence. That's when I noticed I had an ability for telekinesis, but it wasn't strong at the time. And I had an affinity for ghosts."

He smiled. "Ghosts?"

"Yes. They seemed to be attracted to me. I guessed they sensed the magic in me, even if I didn't yet realize it was there."

"Incredible," he whispered. His eyes were boring into mine like drill bits. He truly was an attractive vampire, if you liked the look of a mature man of the world.

"When did you first realize you were a witch?" he asked.

"My parents—adoptive parents—forbade any talk of magic or witchcraft. I was not allowed books about it or to watch movies or TV shows involving it. I didn't find out until years later that my biological parents, who had died when I was a baby, were both witches. Since the topic of magic wasn't allowed, I was naturally curious about it. It wasn't until I went off to college that I bought some books and tried some spells. I joined a small group of Wiccans. But look at me—talking about myself too much. Tell me about yourself."

"No, please, I want to hear more about you."

I was enjoying telling my story. Few people—especially men—were willing to listen. He was special in that way.

"When I went to nursing school and got my first job, magic moved to the back burner. Later, I tinkered with it again, exploring spells to reduce stress. After my husband left me—"

"Impossible! How could a man ever leave you?"

"He was gay. And later was turned into a vampire." I left out the part about him getting staked by cops.

"Ah, so your experience with vampires runs deep."

"Yes," I said. "As one of the few humans who knows you folks truly exist, it was easy for me to get a job as a home-health nurse for supernatural creatures."

"But why would you want to do that?"

"I'd been working in the Intensive Care Unit for years. It finally got to me. Too much stress and heartache. Too many extra shifts. So much—"

Suddenly, Humbert was sitting next to me on the sofa. He had moved so quickly I didn't even see it.

An alarm bell rang in my head, but it was muffled. With Humbert an inch from my right side, I felt his powerful strength, his superhuman abilities. It was a vibe that quickened my heart.

Feelings of arousal grew in me. Maybe it was pheromones, but this gentleman exuded sexiness and desire. His charms made me lightheaded. And now his thigh was touching mine.

"Tell me more about how you felt," he whispered close to my ear.

Warmth rose from deep inside me. I desired him. No, I shouldn't. Yes, I must.

His finger traced a line down my thigh.

In the back of my head, a voice told me this guy was a cheese ball and how could I allow myself to fall for this stereotypical seduction?

The voice shouted that he was mesmerizing me.

I grabbed both charms through my blouse with my left hand and moved a few inches away from him, trying to slow down my breathing.

"There is nothing wrong with enjoying what we want," he whispered.

That mental alarm bell, previously muffled, was now clanging at full volume. I quickly prepared a simple protection spell to surround my body as I stood.

"Let's get back to the matter at hand," I said in a thick voice. "Do you want the spell, and will you leave Courtney alone?"

"Why would I want Courtney when I have before me such an enchanting woman? So beautiful. So mature."

Yep, he lost me at "mature." Being in my forties did not make me "mature." It made me wise enough, though, to see through his seduction attempt.

I stepped away, out of arm's reach of him.

"Mr. Humbert do not think for one moment that I will be your prey or your conquest. Tell me now if you'll accept our agreement, or you'll have to leave."

He leaped at me before the protection spell was ready,

knocking me to the floor. As I rolled away from him, an amulet brushed his chest, and he hissed with pain.

But he kept up his attack. He seized my arms and held them to the floor while his jaws pushed between my shoulder and head, trying to reach my neck. I thrashed about with all my strength, but he was overpowering me.

I pounded my knee into his family jewels, and he yelped. Yes, even vampires are vulnerable there.

I got my right arm free and found the power charm in my pocket. It was like a rabbit's foot but was from some other creature I didn't want to know about. The charm had been infused with power and magic for years before I acquired it, and I used it like a booster for my spells when needed.

Right now, I needed it very badly.

I pumped more power into the protection spell and felt its shielding bubble form inches from my skin.

The vampire's head struck at my neck like a snake, but I somehow blocked it with my shoulder. Pain flared in my shoulder from his fangs.

He struck again, but this time recoiled as if he had smashed into a wall.

The protection bubble had worked.

Next, I quickly chanted the words to a warding spell, designed to drive evil away from me.

He stopped attacking.

"I see you no longer are in the mood," he said as he got to his feet.

I jumped to my feet as well. "I was never in the mood. You were mesmerizing me. That's not seduction; it's rape. Just like putting a drug in my drink."

"You don't know what you're missing." He leered at me with hate in his eyes.

"Get out and never come back," I said.

The warding spell pushed him toward the door, gradually at first, like a border collie herding him. Then, like the collie biting him on the butt.

"Tell Courtney I'll be seeing her soon," he said as he leaped across the threshold, and I slammed the door behind him.

CHAPTER 4
DESTROYED

Three nights later, my phone rang at 2:30 a.m., awakening me from a deep sleep. It was Beatrice.

"I'm a human, Beatrice. And I don't keep vampire hours anymore."

"Have you heard?"

"Heard what?"

"Hugh Humbert has been murdered. He was staked in his bed last night. Agnes found his remains and a metal rod impaling his bed."

"Oh, my."

"You never told me if he accepted your offer to leave the human woman alone."

"No, he didn't accept. He also tried to mesmerize and attack me, but my magic saved me. The world is better off without him, I have to say."

"Never repeat that."

"Why not?" I asked before I realized the answer.

"The HOA wants to find his murderer. Jellyfish Beach doesn't have a ruling council of vampires, and we like it that way. But it means when a crime is committed, we have to find the culprit ourselves. Don't carelessly say things that could cast suspicion on you."

"You don't believe that I did it, do you?"

"Of course not. I think Humbert's human girlfriend did it out of desperation."

"So, if she did do it, what would happen to her? Vampires don't have the authority to punish humans."

"We don't need the authority. We just do it. We have our own Policing Committee. Usually, we prosecute vampire-on-vampire crime, but we reserve the right to punish any creature that harms one of us. Humans wouldn't let their own kind be killed by vampires, would they?"

"Um, actually, we do all the time. How do you punish humans?"

"Let's just say their blood does not go to waste."

I realized that now, instead of protecting our client from one vampire, I had to save her from an entire building's worth of them.

"Do you have any good news for me?" Courtney asked that evening at the botanica.

"Ha!" Luisa exclaimed.

"What? Is something wrong?"

"Mr. Humbert was murdered," I said, my eyes locked on hers, searching for a reaction.

Her eyes welled with tears, and she convulsed with sobs.

Frankly, I did not expect this reaction.

"Did your magic kill him?" she asked me in between sobs. "You didn't have to use such a powerful spell. All he had was a blood intolerance."

"It could have been an allergy," Luisa said.

"He had to lock himself in the bathroom for half the night. But it's not as if it were fatal."

"If it was an allergy, it could be fatal," Luisa said.

"He didn't have anaphylaxis from an allergic reaction. And the spell didn't kill him," I said. "I didn't even cast the spell. He refused the offer."

I thought it best not to mention that Humbert also tried to mesmerize me and feed on me. No sense in upsetting Courtney any further.

"I just wanted him to free me," she said, sniffling and wiping her eyes with a tissue Luisa gave her. "He wasn't a bad person."

He was a cold-hearted predator—which all vampires are—with none of the redeeming qualities many of them have.

"Aren't you going to ask how he died? Maybe you already have first-hand knowledge," Luisa said.

Courtney froze. "You're implying I killed him?"

"The more accurate term is 'destroyed him,'" I said. "Technically, he wasn't alive, being a vampire and all."

They both ignored me.

"I could never have killed him."

"You wanted to get out of an abusive relationship," Luisa said. "Happens all the time."

"Why would I come to you two for help if I was going to destroy him?"

"To deflect suspicion from yourself," Luisa said. "Or maybe it was just a spur-of-the-moment crime of passion."

"Why are you acting like a cop? I thought you were a spiritual advisor."

"I guess I watch too many cop shows."

Courtney turned to me. "How did he die?"

"He was staked in his bed."

Courtney shuddered. "Like in the movies?"

I nodded. "The legends are correct. Though the stakes don't have to be wooden. Metal works, too."

"Did anyone call the police?" Courtney asked.

"The police can't get involved in supernatural crimes," I said. "No one is supposed to know vampires truly exist. *You* shouldn't know, in fact. Mr. Humbert broke all sorts of rules when he shared his secret with you."

"But why?"

"It would knock the world off its axis if people knew how prevalent the supernatural is all around us. There would be mass panic. Religions would be disrupted. And the supernatural creatures would be hunted down and exterminated."

"The only way supernatural creatures can avoid being persecuted is to remain hidden," Luisa explained.

"Some humans know about supernaturals," I said. "And some of these humans are hostile. Innocent supernaturals have been murdered by these individuals."

"We try to protect them," Luisa said.

"So, to answer your question, the police can't know about Mr. Humbert. The vampire community will try to find the culprit and deliver their own form of justice."

"And it won't be pretty," Luisa added.

"I think whoever did it should be punished," Courtney said.

"You realize the vampires are going to suspect you, right?" Luisa asked.

Courtney's lips parted slightly. She looked dumbfounded.

"But I'm innocent."

"I'm afraid there are some members of Humbert's community who know about you," I said.

"Hugh told me he's dated other humans."

"You're the most recent. And they know you weren't happy in the relationship."

"How do they know that last part?"

My stomach dropped. "I'm sorry. I mentioned it to a vampire. She wasn't a fan of his and was eager to help you get away from him."

"But now the vampires will suspect me. Do they have an actual police force?"

"No," I replied. "Just volunteers."

"Are they fair and objective?"

"They try to be." I didn't mention that I didn't know of any cases in which they investigated a human for a crime against vampires.

I also didn't mention that their punishments would be brutal. Vampires are not queasy about killing.

"We can help you," I said.

"Let me get this straight: I was paying you to get Hugh to leave me alone. Someone murders him, and because of your loose lips, the vampires suspect me. So, now I've got to pay you to clear my name?"

"Correct," Luisa said.

"They would suspect you even without my loose lips," I said. It was true, but now I felt terribly guilty for having mentioned her.

"What can these vampires legally do to me?"

"They don't care about the law," Luisa said. "Or the living."

Courtney swallowed. "How much do you charge for this kind of thing?"

"The same hourly rate I was going to charge you for my time creating the spell and trying to persuade Humbert," I said. "Though we'll give you a generous discount."

Luisa glared at me.

"How many hours will this take?" Courtney asked.

"I don't know," I admitted. "We're kind of new to this. But I understand vampires better than any human in this town does, I can confidently say."

Courtney nodded as she thought it over.

"How did I get myself into this mess?" she thought aloud.

"You hooked up on a dating app with a guy who claimed he was a vampire," Luisa said. "That should have sent up warning flares, even if you thought he was lying."

"Yeah." Courtney nervously twisted a lock of hair. I got the feeling she didn't normally wear it short like this. Maybe she was trying to present herself as more mature and sophisticated than she really was.

"Please help me," she said. "We'll talk about the fee later. I don't want any vampires coming after me. In fact, I'll be happy if I never see a vampire again."

"Yes, because they'll want to kill you," Luisa said.

This time, *she* was the recipient of *my* glare.

❦

AFTER COURTNEY LEFT THE BOTANICA, Carl wandered into the shop. I was glad that Courtney missed seeing him, because one look at Carl would tell you he's a zombie. Wearing his funeral suit as always, the tall, lumbering guy looked, well, dead.

He was Haitian and probably had a dark complexion when he was alive. But now he was almost as pale as a vampire. Unlike a vampire, he was—and I have no politically correct way to put this—slightly decomposed. The voodoo sorcerer who raised him from the dead shouldn't have waited so long to do it. I won't get too graphic, but the skin of his bald head wasn't all there, and neither was his nose. Poor guy. He was probably kind of cute back in the day.

"What do you want, Carl?" Luisa asked. "Did Madame Tibodet send you here on an errand?"

He nodded and grunted. His capacity for speech was lost.

Carl turned away from us and wandered down the aisle where the voodoo supplies and accessories were kept.

"I wish Monique would come here herself and not send Carl on her errands," Luisa said. "I mean, how did he travel here without getting unwanted attention?"

I looked out the window and saw a car idling in the parking lot with the decal of a popular ride-sharing service.

"She ordered him a Guber," I said. "When I use them, I never talk to the driver, so I may as well be a zombie, too."

Luisa shook her head in exasperation.

The sound of a crash came from the aisle. We both jumped and peered down it. A ceramic mortar and pestle for grinding magical ingredients lay broken on the floor.

"Carl! Be careful," Luisa scolded.

He moaned with shame and waved his arms, sending several bottles of purification potions to their destruction.

"You're gonna make the gods angry at you."

For the first time, I noticed a piece of paper pinned to his suit coat. I approached him and read the note. Carl smelled a bit ripe today.

"Oh, Madame Tibodet needs a bag of shark teeth. She said to put it on her account."

"We need to set up online ordering and delivery," Luisa muttered as she took a small plastic bag from beneath the counter and handed it to the zombie.

He moaned his thanks and shuffled from the store, getting into the Guber car outside.

"Okay, back to business," I said. "We need to strategize how we're going to help Courtney."

"I'm just a shopkeeper and santera. You're the vampire expert and amateur detective."

"I'm no detective," I said.

"You solved the murder case with the ghouls. For a former nurse, you make a good detective. You know, our contract with the Friends of Cryptids Society says we're obligated to help exonerate innocent monsters—not humans accused of killing them. We don't have to help Courtney. Even though we can always use the extra cash."

"We promised to help her, but I think we're both in over

our heads. We need to find the actual vampire destroyer and prove to the homeowners' association that he—or she, or it—did it before they arrest Courtney."

"How do we do that?"

"Check out any other vampires or humans who had a motive for destroying Humbert. Unfortunately, I think there are many. There are other women he's mesmerized, like Courtney, and forced to date him. And I gather he defrauded more than one vampire through his wealth-management company."

"Great," Luisa said with sarcasm. "That sounds like a full-time job, and we have a shop to run here."

"I'm less valuable here than you are. After all, you owned the place for years before I came along. I'll take on the brunt of the investigative work," I said, knowing I could convince Matt to help me. Also, I felt guilty for telling Beatrice too much about Courtney, thus putting her on the Policing Committee's radar.

"You'd better hurry. Courtney looks guilty, even to me."

"Me, too," I admitted.

CHAPTER 5
UNDER SUSPICION

Here I was, showing up at Squid Tower for a very different kind of visit, far from the normal requests to perform an undead health screening or irrigate a clogged vampire ear. I was here to exonerate our client by investigating a crime. It wasn't familiar territory for a nurse.

Bernie, the night gate guard, gave me a warm welcome as he let me in, accidentally clipping the rear of my car when he lowered the gate arm. Bernie wasn't the brightest bulb in the box, and after years on the job, he still made this mistake frequently.

At times like this, I was happy to be driving an old wreck with enough miles on it to have circled the globe ten times. I used three different magic spells on it each month just to keep it running.

I parked in the visitor's lot and walked past the pickleball courts, filled with vampires who were paler than their tennis whites. The shuffleboard courts were crowded, as well.

Someone had forgotten to turn on the overhead lights, but, of course, the vampires had no problem seeing in the dark.

All the residents in this retirement community were in their sixties or older in terms of their body ages—preserved for eternity to appear to be the age their bodies had been when they'd been turned. Some had been turned fairly recently, but most had been vampires for decades or even centuries. Agnes, whom I was here to visit, had existed for over 1,500 years.

A bulletin board hung in the lobby of the residential tower. On it was a list of the nightly activities.

9:00 p.m.: a workshop on mesmerization techniques. Many of the residents got their meals from the blood-donation bus, so their human-hunting skills were rusty.

10:00 p.m.: a seminar on interior design for crypts.

11:00 p.m.: Zumba class.

Midnight: arts and crafts in the studio, as well as bridge and canasta in the card room.

1:00 a.m.: water aerobics at the pool.

2:00 a.m.: minuet dance lessons, for those who didn't know how to dance the minuet when they were human during the eighteenth century but wanted to learn now.

3:00 a.m.: the creative-writing workshop I taught for a little extra cash, though it wasn't enough pay for the agonizing prose I had to endure.

Many people discover new interests and talents in retirement; at Squid Tower, you can forget about the talents.

I took the elevator up to Agnes's ocean-view condo. She and Beatrice waited for me in the living room decorated with tasteful antiques.

"Thanks for meeting us here," Agnes said, after giving me a

quick hug. The diminutive Visigoth princess only came up to my chest.

"Here at Squid Tower, we team up our resources for fighting crime," Beatrice explained. "As the oldest vampire of us all, Agnes is the chair of the Policing Committee."

Vampires are very keen on hierarchy, with complicated organizational charts for everything from the HOA to the Movie Club. In contrast, the werewolves who lived next door in Seaweed Manor preferred chaos and impulsiveness. When they fought crime, it was usually with vigilante reprisals.

"Would you like some tea, dear?" Agnes asked.

"No thanks. I'm good."

I make a point of never accepting food or drink from vampires. I don't want to feel like I owe them sustenance in return. If you know what I mean.

Agnes and Beatrice sat side by side on an ornate nine-teenth-century sofa of carved wood and red velvet.

"Tell us, my dear," Agnes said, locking my eyes with an icy stare. "Did you do it?"

I was gob smacked. "Did I really hear you ask that?"

"You were the last human to be with Mr. Humbert," Beatrice said. "And he tried to mesmerize and prey upon you. You were also charging a client to keep him away from her."

"That's absurd! I would never have destroyed him."

"You've destroyed vampires before," Agnes said. "Admittedly, they deserved it. But I'm just pointing out that you are capable of staking one of us."

"You said I was the last human to see him. What makes you so certain a human did it?" I asked.

"Vampires rarely stake vampires," Beatrice said. "Unless it's a community-supported execution."

"You said yourself there are vampires who have motives," I said. "Humbert defrauded many victims of millions of dollars."

"And there are many ways for vampires to kill their own kind without staking them."

"So, are you guys really saying that I'm your primary suspect?"

Agnes, who was so short her feet didn't touch the floor while seated, scooted off the sofa and came over to pat my hand.

"Dear, we are quite fond of you and don't want to believe you did this. We are simply being methodical. We can't rule you out simply because we like you."

"You could try."

"Tell us the entire story, from when you were contacted by your client to when Mr. Humbert showed up at your home."

I recounted the whole thing, and as I did so, it became more and more obvious that Courtney was a much more likely suspect than I. After all, she was the one who wanted to get rid of Humbert. I didn't want to throw her under the bus, but I wanted the two women to come to the same conclusion about her.

"Why you would suspect me is baffling," I said.

Agnes made a clucking sound. "We never said that."

"We want to *eliminate* you as a suspect," Beatrice said.

"How does this work?" I asked. "I mean, your policing and justice system?"

"The Vampire Policing Committee interviews suspects and witnesses," Agnes explained. "We have retired law-enforcement professionals living here who take part and guide us regarding forensics. When we have enough evidence, we charge a suspect with the crime and have a trial before the committee."

"Don't tell me you allow vampires to run around with their guns and terrorize the place?"

"No. We don't ask them to play soldier."

"What happens if the accused is found guilty?"

Agnes and Beatrice looked at each other uncomfortably.

"We'll see about that," Agnes said.

"You mean you've never found anyone guilty before?"

Agnes sighed. "Certainly, never of murder. Most 'crimes' in our community are infractions of the HOA bylaws. Those result in fines, or for the more serious transgressions, banishment. Once, we had to resort to capital punishment."

She referred to the most serious breach of HOA rules, when a resident hung unauthorized holiday decorations on her door and wouldn't take them down. Her punishment was staking.

"What about property crimes or physical assaults by residents?" I asked.

"Same thing: fines or banishment. Occasionally, we let vampires with a dispute fight it out. Rather brutal and messy, but effective."

"What about when humans commit crimes?"

The two vampires looked uncomfortable again.

"There's an occasional burglary, but that's rare," Beatrice said. "We have involved the Jellyfish Beach Police before, but only if it's a crime that won't reveal we're vampires."

"Usually, we don't need to call the police," Agnes said. "The homeowner takes care of it."

A chill went through my scalp when I realized it didn't end well for those burglars. I dreaded asking my next question, but I hadn't gotten a straight answer when I asked Beatrice before.

"If you find a human guilty of staking Humbert, what exactly will be the punishment?"

"You don't want to know."

"That's why we don't want there to be any suspicion of you, dear," Agnes said, patting my hand again.

⁂

"IT'S HIGHLY unusual for us to allow a human to do this," Beatrice said.

"I appreciate it," I said as I followed her and Agnes into Humbert's condo, thanks to the spare key Agnes had. "Even though I'm working for a human client, I want the same thing as you—to find Humbert's murderer."

"You're a nurse and a witch. No background in law enforcement?"

"She's a particularly clever witch," Agnes said. "The more good minds involved in solving this, the better."

To be honest, I was underwhelmed by Humbert's place. A small, dingy two-bedroom, it hadn't been updated since the building was constructed in the 1960s. Despite all the money he allegedly stole, he obviously didn't spend any here.

"I don't understand the vampires in this community who keep their hurricane shutters closed year-round," I said.

"Even if you have heavy drapes, nothing guarantees darkness better than shutters."

"But then you can't enjoy the sounds and smells of the ocean at night."

"Humbert had no interest in that," Beatrice said. "All he cared about was money, human women, and blood. That's his bedroom over there."

I entered the dark room that had floor-to-ceiling windows facing the ocean. They were covered, of course, by aluminum shutters. What a waste. The smell of mildew struck me.

The bed was a wooden platform. It was covered with wet, rumpled sheets atop a deflated plastic-like mattress. A metal spear used by spearfishermen impaled the center of it, surrounded by piles of dark-gray ashes that were also wet. They were all that remained of Humbert.

The carpet in the bedroom was soaking wet.

"Where did all this water come from?" I asked. "Wait, don't tell me this is a waterbed."

"Humbert was quite the swinger back in the days when waterbeds were fashionable," Agnes explained. "The flood of water caused by the punctured mattress damaged the condo beneath us. That's why I came in here and discovered his remains. Without the flooding, he might have been here for weeks undiscovered."

"Did anyone look for fingerprints on the spear?" I asked. "Of course, it won't help without access to the police database. Maybe Affird could help with that."

A former detective, Fred Affird was a resident here in the community he had tried so hard to persecute before he was turned. He should lead this investigation, I thought, not the president of the HOA.

"Affird ordered a fingerprint kit from the internet," Agnes

said. "If he finds any prints, he'll break into the police station, or do whatever it takes to access the database."

"It might be a waste of time, though," Beatrice said. "The culprit could be a human without a criminal record."

"Or a vampire," I retorted. "Vampires tend not to get arrested and fingerprinted."

Beatrice and Agnes couldn't bear to be at the crime scene any longer, so they left the condo and waited for me outside the front door. I guessed their suspicion of me was very low if they left me alone at the scene.

I wandered the dark, depressing space, not knowing what clues I should search for.

One thing I did know how to do was cast a simple spell that would detect if magic had been used recently in the condo. When I was a beginner witch, this spell would have been a big production. But with the experience and instinct I now had, casting it was a breeze.

No, there had been no magic in here recently. Specifically, no black magic—which is what you'd need to kill someone in cold vampire blood.

I continued wandering from room to room, not finding any objects that stood out as potentially left behind by an intruder. There were no muddy footprints or bloody handprints. Also, the place didn't look like it had been roughly searched by an intruder looking for something. Humbert's wallet still sat on his dresser, seemingly untouched by anyone else. And I wasn't going to touch it.

The second bedroom was his office, a dreary one with only a desk, a chair, and a half-empty bookcase. No art on the walls. A laptop computer sat on the desk, open. I touched the keyboard and the words, "Access denied," appeared on the screen. Had someone tried to search the computer?

I closed the laptop and took it along with its charger. Hopefully, Agnes would allow me to take the computer to Matt, who had a techie friend who would know how to get past its security. Evidence of financial fraud could point to specific suspects.

Finally, I took Humbert's business card from a stack on the desk. It read, "Humbert Wealth Management. For clients who invest for eternity." I would call the number and see if Humbert employed any assistants I could speak to.

As I left, I asked Agnes if I could borrow the computer and explained why.

"Yes, but you must share with us any clues you find."

"Is that a wise idea?" Beatrice asked her. "No offense to Missy, but she's still under some suspicion."

"Humbert only worked with vampire clients, so nothing about Missy will be on that computer. I'm reasonably certain that there isn't a single vampire here who could hack into it like Missy's friend. Many of our residents were turned before electricity was invented and can barely operate their televisions."

Before I went downstairs, I offered my condolences for losing a member of their community. They thanked me.

"I didn't like him, but it's chilling to have a fellow vampire destroyed where you live," Beatrice said. "It's humbling to be reminded that we're not as immortal as we think we are."

CHAPTER 6
UNDEAD POETS SOCIETY

B y the time I made it to the lobby, there was little time before my creative-writing workshop was due to begin. I went into the large community room and set up folding chairs in a half circle facing the one where I would sit.

As I was finishing, a vampire entered whom I didn't recognize. He was large, with a huge mane of wild white hair and a long, thick white beard. He looked like Moses.

"Is this the writing workshop?"

Make that Moses with a New Jersey accent.

"Yes. You're welcome to join us. Are you new to Squid Tower?"

"Yes. My name is Wade," he said, giving me a limp, deathly cold handshake. "But how can a name represent what is in a man's soul?"

Oh, no. Purple-prose alert. I could already tell this guy's writing was going to be over the top.

44

"I'm Missy. Please take a seat while I put out an extra chair. What brings you to Squid Tower?"

"The Florida weather, of course. I was in poor health when I was turned, and scores of winters later, I said no more."

"I used to be a home-health nurse for vampires and other supernaturals. It's not my full-time job anymore, but I'm still certified. I continue to see a few patients and would be happy to make an appointment with you to look at what's bothering you."

"I was wondering why a human was running this workshop. Though you are a mortal, I respect and honor you."

I hoped that meant he would not try to feed on me.

"What do you like to write?" I asked.

"Mostly poetry, though I've also penned fiction, essays, reviews. I had a stroke before I was turned. Though vampirism has improved my condition immensely, I haven't put pen to paper in more than a century. I wanted to sit in on your workshops and see if my soul would be stirred enough to inflame my imagination again."

"None of the writing you're going to hear tonight will stir your soul, I'm afraid."

Soon, the members of the class wandered in, clutching electronic notebooks and paper ones, or printed-out short stories. They glanced at him curiously.

"Good evening, everyone," I said. "Introduce yourselves to Wade, our newest member."

They all did so one by one and seemed impressed by his charisma.

"I live just down the hall from you," Sol said. "Sorry I haven't introduced myself earlier."

"Do not apologize, my good man. We have much time ahead of us to swap stories about our lives and adventures."

After they were all seated, I turned to our new member sitting at the end of the half circle.

"Wade, since you're new, you don't have to read anything tonight. Unless you brought something you'd like to share."

"Oh, but I did. This is from a work I wrote long ago. I self-published it in 1855."

"Ha! That means he couldn't get a publisher 'cause it stinks," Leo Schwartz said. I had only recently accepted him into the class and had been afraid of behavior like this.

"That wasn't nice," I scolded. "Please go ahead, Wade."

He jumped to his feet. None of the vampires here ever bothered to stand while reading. He didn't have any notes, but recited from memory:

"I sing the body electric, the armies of those I love engirth me, and I engirth them, they will not let me off till I—"

"I'm sorry to interrupt, Wade. But that's a Walt Whitman poem. We don't allow plagiarism here."

"Do not apologize for recognizing good poetry," he said as he sat down with a mischievous smile.

While the rest of the group went through a tortured description of a childhood cat, a smutty romance scene, a heroic World War II battle, and a weepy tribute to a vampire maker, I kept glancing at Wade.

I'll be darned if he didn't look just like Walt Whitman. Much more so than Moses.

If I remembered correctly, Whitman died in New Jersey in the late 1800s and was buried there.

What if he was undead, instead of dead?

After I had suffered through the awkward prose and the tone-deaf critiques of each story, I waited until the vampires filed out before I stopped Wade.

"Is Wade your real name?"

"As I said before, how can a name label one's true soul?"

"Are you Walt Whitman?"

He laughed. "I'm Wade Winkle, from Camden, New Jersey."

I didn't believe him. When I got home, I got on the internet and searched for info on Walt Whitman. The black-and-white photos of Whitman, particularly those from his later years, looked an awful lot like Wade Winkle.

But why Walt Whitman would want to live at Squid Tower, I had no idea.

⬓⬓⬓⬓

"Hello, may I please speak to Hugh Humbert?" I asked in my most world-weary voice after calling the number on the business card I'd taken from the condo.

The company's business hours were 9:00 p.m. to 5:00 a.m. So, I was fairly confident the young woman who answered the phone was a vampire like her boss.

"Uh, um, he's not available at the moment. Are you a client?"

"No," I said. "I'm an investigator trying to find out who staked him."

She gasped.

I was taking a risk, but trying to bluff my way in by posing as a vampire investor would not work. This assistant now knew her boss had been destroyed and her job was about to end. I was counting on her needing to vent.

I didn't know if vampires could sense if someone else was a vampire over the phone, but I wanted to keep it secret that I was a human. I figured she'd be more open to me that way.

I introduced myself. She said her name was Heather.

"I'm sorry for his passing," I said.

"I thought he would be here for me forever. I thought the undead were invincible."

It was none of my business, but she made me curious. "Were you recently turned?"

"You can tell just by my voice? Yes, I was. Hugh was my maker."

"I'm sorry."

"It's not like he was there for me when I was turned. He dated me, then turned me, then turned his back on me. Forgive me for giving you too much information."

"Not at all. Please continue. Anything you tell me could end up being helpful."

"Instead of being there for me while I suffered through the transformation, he went after new human women. While I was suffering physically and practically going out of my mind, he wasn't there to comfort me and tell me what to expect. I lost my job and had to cut off contact with my family. I lost my apartment, and he gave me some cash, but it wasn't enough to get me back on my feet. All I could afford was a vampire-family's guest house. The only thing he offered me was a job working for him as his assistant, administering his clients' funds."

"Has he turned others?"

"I know there were women before me. It was a thrill for him. Dating humans wasn't enough. Feeding on them wasn't enough. He loved to drain them to the point of death and bring them back as vampires. I think he was addicted to the power."

"Do you know if any of these women would want to stake him?" I asked, though I was speaking to one who would make a good suspect.

"No one specifically."

"He never received any threats?"

"None that I know of."

"I have heard accusations he defrauded some clients. Were you aware of this?"

"I'm not saying anything that could get me in trouble."

"You deny he did this?"

"He may have on his own. I had nothing to do with it."

"I'm trying to learn if any disgruntled clients would want to stake him," I said, trying to move her away from the defensiveness.

"There are a few former clients who would wish him harm, yes. I can't legally tell you their names, except for one of them. This one tried to get relief through some vampire committee, but it went nowhere. Then, he sued Hugh in court. It's a matter of public record now, so I can give you his name. Igor Stanisloopsky."

Now, *that* was a good vampire name.

"How can I reach him?"

"I doubt you can get through to him by calling or emailing. Let me see if his address is in the system. Um, no, just a P.O. box."

She gave me the address, but I knew mailing a letter to him would go nowhere. I'd have to find him another way.

"Thank you for your help. Again, my condolences."

I COULDN'T USE magic to find Igor Stanisloopsky. The spells I knew required me to have a possession of his, or at least know what he looked like. So, I had to resort to the magic of the internet.

As to what he looked like, the search engines didn't find any photos of him, only a Russian hockey player in Canada and a physical therapist in Des Moines. The property appraiser's website didn't have any records under his name; the property he owned was probably under the name of a corporation or trust.

The county public records website scored a hit. There was a notice of the lawsuit. And on it was the name of his attorney. Normally, I wouldn't expect an attorney to divulge the information I needed. But this wasn't just any attorney.

It was Paul Leclerc, werewolf and popular lawyer for vampires who couldn't appear in court during daylight hours and for all supernatural creatures who needed to hide their natures. Paul and I were on friendly terms—enough so, I hoped, that he would cross the line of attorney-client privilege and help me talk to Igor.

"No, you don't want to speak with Igor," Paul said over the phone.

"Why not?"

"He's bad news. An old-school horror-movie vampire. He makes Vlad the Impaler look like a sissy."

"It sounds to me like he might be a good suspect for the slaying of Humbert."

"He would never stake anyone himself. He would have a henchman do it. But I didn't say that."

"You're only making me more curious."

"My client wants to destroy Humbert—but only in the financial and reputational sense. On the record, I can say with confidence that he wouldn't stake the slimy little fraudster. We have a good lead on where Humbert might have hidden a big stash of ill-gotten gains. Why would Igor engage in violence?"

"Anger from the loss of face."

"Well, Igor does have quite a temper."

"Could you please set up a meeting with him?"

"Why would he want to meet with you?"

"To clear his name. The Vampire Policing Committee is pretty amateurish, but even they will recognize that Igor is a likely suspect. Regardless of what's going on in the courts, it's conceivable that an old-school vampire like him would take justice into his own hands."

"Okay, okay, I'll speak with him and see what he says. No guarantees."

"Tell him I have some spells that are great for vampire digestive issues, if he ever needs them."

"I will. Say, you don't happen to have any for werewolf stomach problems, do you?"

"I'll be happy to set up a consultation with you and create a spell. But I must remind you to not eat just meat. You need some fiber in your diet."

Later that day, Paul called me back. He said he was pleased to inform me that Igor was willing to meet with me at his mansion that evening.

He was shocked the vampire agreed to do it.

CHAPTER 7
VAMPIRE CAPITALIST

The richest residents of Jellyfish Beach lived in mansions on the beach. The next tier of wealth lived in homes on the Intracoastal Waterway or Lake Algae. Simply put, the priciest, most-desirable properties were on the water, to heck with hurricanes and floods.

Possibly the wealthiest local resident of all bucked this trend. Igor Stanisloopsky lived far to the west of town on a large piece of property near a nature preserve, with his only neighbors being nurseries, vegetable farms, and alligators.

"Since when have houses built in the Transylvanian style been in Florida?" Matt asked as we rolled along a winding driveway through a swampy area with cypress trees. He had insisted on coming along for my safety.

"I think Florida has other old homes with Gothic features," I said.

There were no lights along the twisting sandy road, so we had to depend on my headlights to navigate our way.

"Wait, it's not Halloween season, is it?"

Matt was referring to the two skeletons hanging from trees on either side of the drive. They looked authentic.

"No. Maybe they're for scaring away salesmen and Jehovah's Witnesses."

"Well, they're working on me."

We passed a rusty metal bear trap. Fortunately, nothing was in it.

"You've got to be kidding!" Matt pointed to the left. "A graveyard? Really?"

Yes, we passed a small plot with stone grave markers. It was overgrown with weeds.

"It's probably for pets. Since vampires are immortal, they go through a lot of pets. Yeah, a pet cemetery. That's what it is. For sure."

"This property is over the top. Where are the code enforcers?"

"This is an unincorporated area. You can probably do whatever you want with your property." I parked in front of the sprawling three-story mansion, with its bizarre blend of Gothic, Victorian, and art-deco features. "I'm glad you came along. This feels almost like a trap."

"Yeah, we're like the stupid characters in a cheap horror movie, walking right into the madman's lair."

We ascended the wide staircase to the front door. The only illumination came from a lamp with a yellow bulb beside the door. I slapped at a mosquito on the back of my neck.

I rang the doorbell. The chime was a samba tune.

I expected a cadaverous butler to open the door and say, "You rang?"

Instead, a handsome man in his forties with a well-trimmed beard flung open the door. He wore a black T-shirt and slacks and beamed with a big smile.

"Welcome to my little country getaway!" he said exuberantly, as if we were long-lost friends. "You must be the supernatural detective and her assistant."

"I'm not a detective," I said. "I'm a nurse and a witch. I'm just helping with some investigating."

"And I'm not her assistant," Matt said. "Just a friend."

"Just friends—the saddest words ever uttered by a man."

"You got that right," Matt said with a wry smile.

"Come in, come in," Igor said, bowing with a flourish.

We followed him through a two-story-tall foyer into a formal parlor that looked like it had been decorated a century ago.

"Nice place you've got here," Matt said. "Interesting architecture."

"Thank you. When I moved here in the eighteen-nineties, there were no decent homes to choose from. So, I transported sections of my previous homes here. I'm very nostalgic, you see."

And very extravagant, I thought. Moving sections of multiple homes must have cost a fortune. This vampire obviously had money to burn, and that's exactly what Humbert did to it.

Matt and I sat in two overstuffed wing chairs. A cat rubbed against my legs. I reached down to pet it and yanked back my hand in alarm.

The creature had the head of a cat, but the body of a dog —a brown and white spaniel of some sort. Its tail wagged with friendliness, but the cat studied me with a neutral expression.

"Mind if I take a picture of your . . . pet?" I asked. "I document unusual species."

"Go right ahead. Would you folks like any refreshments? My human servant makes mango smoothies she says are delicious. The fruit is from trees on the property. May I serve you some?"

He stood before us, so eager to please.

So good-looking, too. I'd never found vampires to be attractive—without being mesmerized. It's probably because I've only dealt with geriatric ones.

"Nothing for me, thanks," Matt replied.

"I'm good, thanks for offering," I said. "We only want to ask you a few questions, and then we'll get out of your lair. I mean, hair."

He cackled delightedly at my Freudian slip. He had jet-black hair, parted on the side, with no signs of mousse. His face was intelligent, with a narrow nose and delicate chin. His build was thin, but the tight black T-shirt showed off how well-defined his chest and abs were.

Matt was staring at me with a frown. He must have noticed my eyes drinking in Igor.

Our host sat across from us in the middle of a sofa, leaning forward with his hands on his knees.

"Fire away with your questions."

"Hugh Humbert's assistant told me you lost a lot of money because of him."

"Is a hundred million a lot? I suppose for most people, yes. I must be the number one suspect in his staking, right?"

I was caught off guard. "Not necessarily. Now, to be clear, did he lose it through bad investment choices?"

"No, he flat out stole it. He disappeared for a while. I heard he went to Iceland, which is really popular among vampires lately."

"It seems foolish of him to return to Florida," Matt said.

"I could have arranged for him to be staked no matter where in the world he was. He must have blown through the money and had to come home."

"That's a lot of money to blow," I said.

"I know vampires who have lost more through gambling addictions."

"Vampires like to gamble?" Matt asked.

"We have an unhealthy tolerance for risk. Comes from being immortal and having preternatural healing abilities, in my opinion."

Igor turned to look at me. He had blue eyes, and I wanted to go swimming in them.

Wait, I must be careful not to be mesmerized.

"Mr. Stanisloopsky—"

"You can call me Igor."

"Igor, how angry are you at Hugh Humbert? Enough to stake him?"

"You're very direct. I like that quality. Now, that's a tricky question. I was furious at him—for a while, at least. However, I don't act according to emotions like anger. If I staked him, it would be for a more rational reason, such as his existence being unworthy of continuing."

This wasn't going the way I had expected. I had planned to ask general questions that eventually pinned him down, while he would attempt to avoid any impression of guilt. Then, I would analyze his behavior and judge if he was lying.

Igor didn't seem to care if I thought he was guilty.

"Did you stake him?" I asked.

"Ah, your directness again. Unfortunately, I won't answer you. It's more fun to keep you guessing."

"Is that because I'm a human?"

"No. My sources tell me you are consulting with the Squid Tower Policing Committee. I don't fear them. They're amateurs who only have authority within their private community. They don't have the right to penalize me or regulate my behavior. If there was an absolute ruler of vampires in Florida, or in Crab County, things might be very different."

Not regulating independent vampires like Igor was a big problem for the vampire community. If he was indiscreet, his hunting could attract attention from the human police—and possibly the public at large—putting all vampires at risk of discovery and destruction.

"Even if you're not forced to follow rules, it's not a bad idea," I said. "In the interest of keeping the vampire population secret."

"That is why I live at the edge of the Everglades, far from the city centers. There are fewer humans to hunt, but many are migrant farm workers who are easier to disappear."

I glanced at Matt, whose face had turned white.

Igor slapped his knee and laughed uproariously.

"No, I don't prey on farm workers. Although there's no Blood Bus showing up here like at Squid Tower, I do have a meal-delivery service."

"You mean you get a package each week with pints of

blood for each day?" Matt asked. "I use a service like that—but for human food. Who has time to cook? Who has time to hunt?"

"No, a delivery service. I order a pizza. The driver leaves with a tip and two wounds in his neck."

"Oh."

"Just kidding! I will not divulge my feeding habits to the very creatures I prey upon."

Matt's face went a couple of shades whiter. I had given him a vampire-repellant amulet to wear, but it didn't appear to instill confidence in him. Unlike me, he had very little experience interacting with vampires. And that's actually a good thing.

I tried to change the topic back to our main purpose for coming here.

"If we assume you were not the one who staked Mr. Humbert, do you have any ideas about who it might be?"

"His assistant is certainly resentful," Igor said, stroking his cute chin in thought. "Recently turned vampires can be quite sullen regarding their makers. They're like adolescent humans."

"Do you know of any other clients who had brutal losses?"

"I have no access to that information. Vampires love to gossip, though, and I hear he has many other angry ex-clients. The reason you're here tonight is that I happened to have lost the most money. That I know of."

"Okay. Thank you for your time," I said, rising from my chair. "I'll give you one last chance to admit or deny your guilt."

He smiled, revealing a glimpse of fang.

"Why should I make your life easy, when I can make mine

more fun?" He got to his feet. "Come, I want to show you something."

"We should really be going," Matt said.

"Don't you worry, little man. You can come, too."

"Where?" Matt asked.

"You'll see. It's a surprise."

"I don't like to associate vampires with the concept of surprise."

"You will not be harmed, I assure you. I don't get many visitors, and I like to show off my collection. Come on, come on. Don't be scaredy-cats."

He motioned for us to follow him from the parlor. We went down a long hallway covered in oil paintings from different eras. I recognized a Picasso, two Monets, a handful of Rembrandt sketches, and even medieval art. They were all originals.

We passed several rooms, then the hall turned several times at odd angles as we traversed the stitched-together building. Finally, we arrived at a converted four-car garage. The concrete floor was covered with blue indoor-outdoor carpeting and office cubicles. There had to be twenty to thirty men and women—mostly men—wearing headsets and talking on the phone or typing on computers.

"Is this a telemarketing operation?" Matt asked.

"Deceptive telemarketing, loan-collecting, phone scams, email scams, senior exploitation, phishing—every scummy way to make a buck." He giggled. "And I make a lot of bucks."

I was disappointed. When Igor mentioned his "collection," I had feared something horrifying and hoped for something enchanting. Instead, it was just a big scam.

"Do they work for you, or are they mesmerized slaves?" I asked, surprising him again with my directness.

"They're mesmerized!" he cackled with amusement. "This operation is not exactly what you think it is. These aren't the poor wage slaves who work out of necessity for telemarketers and scammers. These were their employers—the scum-of-the-earth entrepreneurs who went into business to steal from innocent people."

"Really?" I asked.

"Absolutely! I received one phishing email too many, and I went ballistic. Using my plentiful resources, I tracked down all these lowlifes, captured them, mesmerized them, and gave them the punishment they so richly deserved. Now, they're forced to do the work others did for them. I keep them enslaved, *and* I feed on them!" He laughed again. "They are my Blood Bus."

There was a certain poetic justice here, but I was still creeped out. Igor must have recognized the look on my face.

"None of these humans ran legitimate companies," Igor added. "All were scammers. They're the worst of the worst."

"I can't argue with you there," Matt said, "but what gives you the right to punish them?"

"Ah, but isn't that the underlying theme of your visit here? Who has the right to punish others in society? Vampire kings? A committee of HOA members? A judiciary made up of humans wearing robes? If you really think about it, only God has the authority to judge us, and he's not here on earth to do it. Well, I am."

"You think you're God?" Matt asked, with a snideness that

surprised me, considering Igor could pop his head off like a dandelion.

Igor giggled. "I don't at all. But I'm stronger and more powerful than humans. And I'm immortal. I'm your next best thing to a god. And these scum buckets"—he pointed to the cubicles—"are suffering my judgment."

Okay, I thought. I do not want to get on his bad side.

I gave Igor an extra-cheery smile on our way out.

CHAPTER 8

PREDATION AND A MOVIE

"Y ou could have tried a little harder to hide your attraction to Igor," Matt said, sulking in the passenger seat.

"I'm not attracted to him. He's a vampire, by criminy!"

"Your pupils expanded when you looked at him. Your eyes were eating up his buff body."

"Maybe he was trying to mesmerize me. Besides, his body is undead. I personally find that gross. I can't for the life of me understand how humans can be attracted to vampires. Just the thought of their cold skin freaks me out."

"Say what you will. I know what I saw."

"Stop acting like a sullen teenager. You know how I feel about you and where we can take our friendship."

"Yeah, and I told you I don't want us to be just friends with benefits. My feelings for you go much deeper than that."

I leaned over, my eyes still on the road, and gave him a quick peck on the cheek.

"We'll save this discussion for a better setting. Let's discuss if Igor's the one who staked Humbert."

"Why was he so cavalier about whether we suspected him? That's not the way someone who's guilty would act."

"Or he's guilty and simply doesn't care if we know it or not," I said, turning onto the main road back to town. "You heard him. Justice is a gray area for him. And we're just lowly humans in his eyes."

"You're an attractive human in his eyes."

"Knock it off. He wasn't flirting with me."

"Whatever." Matt continued to sulk rather than focus on the problem at hand.

"Igor is the most high-profile fraud victim. Heather gave us his name only because he was suing Humbert. There are other victims we don't know about. We need to get their names."

"Are they all vampires?"

"Humbert had only vampires as clients."

"Can we convince Heather to give us more names?"

"Maybe if you flirt with her," I teased.

"Nice try, but I'm not taking the bait."

"I took Humbert's laptop from his condo. Can your friend, Sal, hack into it? We could find client names, maybe threatening emails or more."

"Isn't that illegal?"

"We're in the vampire justice system now. Anything goes if they approve of it. Agnes told me to go ahead."

"Okay, I'll reach out to him."

Matt nodded and texted Sal. "He's cool with that, but he said he can't guarantee he'll be able to get past the security software."

"That's fine. We'll set up a time to do it soon. Right now, I want to speak with Heather again. When I talked to her before, she seemed a little unstable. Which means she might divulge more information than she normally would."

"Wow, aren't you cold and calculating?"

"She's a vampire. You can't find a colder and more calculating predator."

"You don't need to remind me."

I called her. "Heather, it's Missy Mindle again. Do you have any time to talk a little more?"

"Hi." Long pause. "I'm not feeling very chatty tonight."

"Please. It won't take long. I met Igor Stanisloopsky tonight. Quite the character."

"Yes, he is."

"Well, he got me thinking about some things. I truly want to find out who staked Mr. Humbert, and I don't think Igor did it. I just have a few questions I'd like to ask you."

"Yes?"

"My investigative partner and I are driving through town, and I thought it would be easier to talk if we could swing by your place."

Matt made a choking sound and gaped at me in astonishment. I ignored him.

"You know I live with other vampires," Heather said.

"Yes. I've visited vampire nests before. Doesn't bother me."

"It would bother me," Matt said.

I waved my hand to silence him.

"Where do you live?" I asked. "We won't bother you for more than a few minutes."

She didn't answer.

"Please, Heather. We really need your help to solve Mr. Humbert's murder."

"Okay," she said with a sigh before giving me the address. It was in an older suburban neighborhood of Jellyfish Beach.

I told her we'd be there shortly. Then, I called Agnes.

"Oh, hello," she said. "Beatrice and I were just sitting here chatting about the staking."

"Oh, good. Why don't you make this a video call?"

"How do I do that?"

"Press the video button on the menu screen."

Beep, beep, beep-beep.

"I can't figure out how to do it on this darned thing."

"Let me try," said Beatrice in the background.

Beep, beep, beep, beep.

Suddenly, my phone's screen filled with a closeup video of Beatrice's ear.

"Where are you?" she asked. "I don't see anything."

"Hold the phone away from you, so I can see you and Agnes."

Now, I was looking at a closeup view of Beatrice's nose.

"Farther away," I said.

Now, I was looking at Agnes's coffee table.

"This isn't working," I said. "How about if you turn off the camera and turn the speaker on?"

Beep, beep, beep, beep.

"Don't be frustrated," Matt said. "My mother still has problems with her smartphone. And these ladies are hundreds of years older than she is."

"What speaker?" Beatrice said. "There's audio coming out of the phone already."

"Give it back to me," Agnes said in the background. The video ended, but the phone fell and landed hard. "Okay, I've got it now," Agnes said. "Why are you calling?"

"I wanted to give you an update. We spoke to Igor Stanisloopsky tonight. He's the largest fraud victim. Humbert's assistant gave me his name."

"What is she saying?" Beatrice asked in the distance.

"She said she spoke to the largest fraud victim," Agnes relayed to her.

"And I don't believe he's the one who staked Humbert."

Again, Agnes repeated what I said to Beatrice.

"You know, it's easy to put it on speaker," I said, "but never mind. Right now, we're heading to the assistant's home. I'm going to see if I can get more names out of her."

After sharing that with Beatrice, Agnes said, "You be careful, dear. The home of a vampire you don't know is a dangerous place for a human."

"I have Matt with me."

"Your sweetheart? I don't know how much help he'll be."

"We have protection charms," I said. "Don't worry."

"It seems like you're going to a lot of trouble to protect Humbert's human girlfriend. We all think she's the one who did it."

"I know," I said. "But I don't think that's true."

"I certainly hope she's paying you well."

That was a good point. Courtney hadn't paid us anything yet.

"Yeah, don't worry about it. I'll call you if I learn anything new from the assistant."

"That was exasperating," I said to Matt after I'd hung up.

"Seniors will be seniors, even if they have vampire powers."

"At least we'll be like that for only a short time before we shuffle off this mortal coil."

"Assuming we don't get turned. Which you're increasing the odds of happening."

"Keep your amulet touching your body at all times."

"Not very reassuring," Matt grumbled.

We arrived at Heather's address, and I was surprised. It was in a very nice neighborhood. The streetlights were far apart, but each home had porch lights on, giving the tree-lined neighborhood a cheery feel. The last time I'd been to a vampire nest, it had been in an old, rundown home that oozed neglect and nightmares.

The home we were parked in front of was a large Mission-style structure with stucco walls and a barrel-tile roof. It was probably from the 1920s or '30s. Heather said she lived in the quaint guest cottage behind the main house.

As we walked down the driveway, I was surprised to see a trampoline in the backyard. Not exactly common on a vampire's property.

I knocked on the cottage door. Heather opened it with a wild look in her eyes. When she saw me, she retracted her fangs out of politeness.

"I don't know if I should be speaking with you," Heather said. Not much of a welcome.

"We won't take much of your time," I said. "This is Matt, who's helping with my investigation."

"Hi," Matt said. "Why is there a trampoline here?"

"Because Jacob enjoys it."

"And who is Jacob?"

"He's a forty-year-old vampire trapped in a twelve-year-old's body," Heather explained. "You see, the Chambers, who own this property, are your typical nuclear family who happened to be turned together—the two parents and two kids."

"How did *that* happen?"

"All I can say is be careful where you take your family camping."

Matt and I shuddered.

"The Chambers went out tonight for some predation and a movie. It would be best if you left before they return."

"You'll get no argument from me," Matt said.

Heather still stood in the doorway, without having invited us inside.

"Can we please discuss who else might be likely to have staked your boss?" I asked.

"He was more than my boss. I told you, he was my maker."

She broke into tears. Her tears were mixed with blood, which was disconcerting. Helpful tip: try to avoid making a vampire cry.

"I'm sorry," I said. My instinct was to pat her arm to comfort her, but a deeper instinct told me to keep my hand away from the sharp teeth. "We want to find justice for him."

"Who's going to find justice for *me*? All the neglect I suffered after I was turned. All the confusion and fear and self-hatred. I was alone with no one to guide me or care about me. What did Hugh do? He gave me a job doing the stuff he couldn't be bothered to do. To clean up his messes."

"To cover up his crimes?" I dared to ask.

"I didn't cover up his crimes. He deserved to be punished for them. And to be punished for what he did to me!"

"Um, did you, by any chance, punish him?" Matt asked.

Before my eyes could even register it, Heather was no longer in the doorway. The door remained open, but she had disappeared.

"Heather? Where—"

Something hit me like a freight train, and my world went dark.

⚡

I woke up in a Ficus hedge. It took a moment for me to register where I was. As the back of my skull throbbed, I remembered that something had attacked me and knocked me unconscious.

That something must have been Heather, moving with the speed of a vampire. Thank heavens she hadn't torn my head off.

The front door to the cottage was closed. I figured Heather had retreated to her personal space.

But where was Matt?

Pulling myself painfully from the hedge with my hands on the ground, I rolled over on the lawn and looked around for Matt.

Please, don't let him be drained or missing his head.

Please, let Matt be alive.

The lawn was deserted. The night was quiet, except for the hum of distant traffic.

And a *boing-boing-boing* sound.

I got to my feet and looked around the corner of the cottage. There he was, bouncing on the trampoline. No, not playing on it like a kid. His prone, limp body was bouncing on it like he had been dropped from a tremendous height. The trampoline's springs were slowly losing energy.

I rushed over, and as his bouncing subsided, grabbed him in my arms. His neck had a pulse. His chest was rising and falling normally.

"Matt, are you okay?"

His eyes fluttered open.

Then he kissed me. Intensely, like he was in the middle of a naughty dream.

He stopped when he became fully conscious.

"What. The. Heck?" he mumbled in a hoarse voice.

"Heather attacked us, I guess. It happened so fast I didn't see anything."

"You were in front of me, and I saw something blow by and knock you away from the doorway." He rubbed his eyes. "Man, my head hurts. As I was saying, you went flying like a bowling pin. Then, out of nowhere, it came after me."

"Did you see it?"

"Barely."

"Heather?"

"I guess. But she moved so fast, I could barely see her. I'm not sure if it was male or female."

"Be thankful for our vampire-repellant amulets. Without them, we'd have holes in our necks."

Impulsively, I checked my neck with my hands. No puncture wounds.

"If it was Heather, that means she did stake Humbert, right?" Matt asked, finally sitting up on the trampoline.

"I guess so. Not so smart of you to ask her, though."

"You're the detective. I'm just the muscle."

Recalling the sight of him flopping on the trampoline, I laughed.

CHAPTER 9
MONSTER ALERT

"You're certain it was the assistant who attacked you?" Agnes asked me as she and Beatrice sipped drinks at the oceanfront swimming pool.

Yes, retired seniors sipping drinks poolside was the ultimate Florida cliche, but it was different here at Squid Tower. These seniors were basking in the light of the moon, not the sun. And their drinks were not frosty piña coladas, but warm pints of B negative.

Other than that, all things were as you'd expect, with small groups around the pool deck, gossiping in lounge chairs while an elderly man and a woman wearing a bathing cap paddled slowly up and down the pool, doing their exercise laps.

"Who else could it have been, if not Heather?" I asked. "The homeowners were out, and Matt and I were the only ones there besides Heather."

I had dropped Matt off at his bungalow after we'd visited the ER to make sure the blows to our heads hadn't been serious. Matt most definitely did not want to accompany me to Squid Tower. He said he'd had enough of vampires to last him for the rest of his life.

"Describe the attack to me again."

"Heather was standing in her doorway, then suddenly she wasn't. Right after that, I was struck from behind. You vampires can move too quickly for humans to see you. Matt was behind me, and he had only the briefest glimpse of the attacker. He thought it was probably Heather. She was upset and acting unstable when I asked for more names of Humbert's fraud victims."

"Yes, that makes sense."

"Why didn't she kill us?" I asked, though I was afraid to hear the answer.

"She didn't want to get into more trouble than she already was. Killing humans, as you know, is forbidden because of the danger of the authorities discovering a vampire did it. Even if the killing was done in a manner a human murderer would have used. She didn't want to add that to her crime of killing one of her own—the worst crime of all."

The simultaneous sudden intakes of breaths around the swimming pool sounded like a swarm of aroused insects.

"Goodness gracious," Beatrice said.

All the vampires on the pool deck stared at the figure strolling along the concrete walkway toward them.

It was Wade Winkle, aka Walt Whitman.

And he was buck naked. The only thing he wore was his enormous white beard and a goofy grin.

"Good evening, neighbors," he said, waving. "Lovely evening for a swim, is it not?"

He was in pretty good shape for a vampire of his body age.

He dove into the pool and did breast strokes with strength and precision. The woman in the bathing cap, who had been doing laps, squealed, and scurried up the ladder.

Whitman stopped swimming and laughed as he watched her hurry to her lounge chair.

"What's the matter?" he called after her. "Haven't you seen a naked vampire before?"

The man who had been doing laps swam by, making a wide detour around Whitman.

"I always swim naked," Whitman said to him. "My pure body, like one with pure nature. It's exhilarating. It's a tonic for the soul."

"It's perverted," said an onlooker. "Who does he think he is, a hippie?"

"The best-looking hippie I ever saw," Beatrice muttered, unable to take her eyes off the skinny-dipping poet.

"It's no big deal to me," Agnes grumbled. "Our Visigoth warriors swam naked in the river all the time, even while the women were washing clothes. It's a sign of virility. The problem is, Wade didn't shower before getting into the pool. Didn't he read the sign with the rules? We'll have to issue a warning to him. And stop ogling him, Beatrice. You're a married woman."

"Ladies, I best be going," I said. "Will the Policing Committee follow up on the case by tracking down Heather?"

"Of course," Agnes said. "It would be too difficult for you, as a human, to find her. And we would never expect you to be able to capture her."

"I agree. Enjoy the rest of your evening."

"Wait, Missy," Beatrice said. "Are you absolutely sure you're okay after your injury?"

"Yes. Thank you."

"You accomplished a lot. Thank you for your help."

I smiled and said goodnight, while Whitman giggled along with the group of ladies who had jumped into the pool beside him. With their suits on, I should add.

I SLEPT LATE THAT MORNING, exhausted and sore. Luisa was completely supportive when I told her I wouldn't make it to work. I promised her I would open the botanica the following day, so she wouldn't have to.

Contrary to what you might think, we keep brutally long hours, almost as long as a pharmacy's. Because to some customers, that's what we were. With a name like the Jellyfish Beach Mystical Mart and Botanica, you'll be forgiven if you thought it a place that sells crystals and incense for hobbyists.

Yeah, we sell incense, but we also sell products our customers consider indispensable for navigating their lives: figurines of saints, spirits, and gods to help their prayers reach those entities. Potions that give them luck, courage, and wisdom. Charms that keep away evil spirits and, allegedly, diseases. And bug spray to keep away the enemies that are more prevalent than evil spirits.

Because of the people who believe divine intervention cures everything from constipation to colic, we must open early and stay open late. The same goes for the people who need a potion for business success before they commute to work, and for those who need a virility potion before they come home after work.

Since tomorrow would be an early day, and my body hadn't fully adjusted after I gave up working the vampire shift, I was determined to rest today. I fed the cats and read *The Jellyfish Beach Journal* at my kitchen table with my tea and toast. Yes, I still get a physical newspaper delivered. I'm old school, and some of my spells require burning news articles on topics associated with the spells.

My relaxation was soon disturbed by the smell of cigarette smoke.

"Freaking Tony!" I said aloud as I got up from the table and stormed into the garage.

The iguana sat atop my workbench, puffing away on a Camel.

"What did I tell you about smoking in the house?" I demanded.

"I'm not in your house. I'm in the garage," the lizard said. "It's not finished space under air, according to the tax appraiser's office."

"We've already been through this. The smoke seeps in through the laundry-room door. Take your cancer sticks outside."

"How are you going to explain to your neighbors why a four-foot-long iguana is smoking in your yard?"

"I'll tell them it's because you're addicted to nicotine."

"Look, we need to talk."

The problem with animals that can talk is they love to show off their ability.

"About what? You want me to plant more beautiful flowers so you can just eat them?"

"Please, lose the tone. I'm living with you to help you navigate the supernatural world, and you should know there's trouble coming. There's a monster in Jellyfish Beach that's never been here before. I'm not sure yet what it is, but I can sense its presence."

"What does it have to do with me?"

He cocked his head, making the crest atop his head quiver with impatience at my stupid question.

"The Society gave you the responsibility to protect cryptids.. Those wackos, the Knights Simplar, could find this monster and kill it unless you find it first."

He was right. This is the duty I accepted when the Society spent lavishly to prevent the botanica from going bust and to keep Luisa and me gainfully employed as monster monitors.

"How am I supposed to do anything about a monster you can't identify? Do you know where it might be?"

"Sorry. You should be thanking me for sensing it. If you want to know more, you need to use some magic. You're the witch, after all. I'm just a lizard with a nicotine addiction."

"You're a witch's familiar. You helped me with the digestion spell."

"And I'm helping you with my connection to the supernatural world. I can't bail you out every time you need to create a spell."

"You're being petulant because I scolded you for smoking in here."

Tony shrugged and tossed the cigarette butt on the concrete floor.

"Are you serious?" I asked, pointing to the smoldering butt.

He climbed down a leg of the bench and extinguished the butt by swatting it with his tail.

"If I get more information about this creature, I'll let you know. In the meantime, I'm going to eat your neighbor's garden," he said before crawling out the half-open window.

I was tempted to blow off Tony's news about the monster and just chill out for the day. My sense of duty nagged me, though. The Friends of Cryptids Society of the Americas was very serious about their mission. And because I had a feeling there was more to them than met the eye, I figured I should make the effort to search for the monster.

I knew a creature-hunting spell that might work if I could pull it off. Ironically, it had been created by Don Mateo. It was one of the ones he had inscribed in the back of the grimoire he had once owned.

That book had become my most valuable, and valued, spell book, so I kept it hidden. When I wasn't using it regularly, I kept it *very* hidden. It was in the bottom of the cat-litter box, where no sane burglar would want to search. It was safely sealed in two plastic bags, ensconced below a false bottom under the liner of the box. Bubba and Brenda were miffed when they saw me extracting the book from their lavatory.

The spell was developed by Don Mateo in collaboration with the shaman of the indigenous Timucua of Northeast Florida to alert them of invading creatures. The magic they had been using before this one did not work too well, evidenced by the settlement of Spaniards that appeared in 1565 on the Timucuan lands.

The spell worked by broadcasting waves of energy within a

limited geographical area. It synced with the energies, or life forces, of all the organisms that lived in that specific ecosystem. Believe it or not, these energies were on similar frequencies. An organism that was foreign to this ecosystem, and came from one that was drastically different, would emit energy on a different frequency. This would trigger the spell to alert the magician who cast it.

It might sound simple, but it took the rest of the morning for me to prepare for and cast the spell.

I pulverized old rodent bones, trimmed bird feathers, and measured out fifteen different dried herbs and spices. Then, I collected fresh garden soil and palmetto fronds, and blended them with drops of my blood. Finally, I burned them in a bowl made of quartz with the crumpled paper from a newspaper article about invasive species in Florida. It was a topic that appeared in the paper regularly.

And that was the simple part of the spell.

The burning bowl was at the upper point of a pentagram drawn within a large circle on my kitchen floor. Kneeling inside this magic circle, I gathered my internal energies, combined them with the elemental energies of the world around me, and performed the invocation.

I read aloud the Spanish, Latin, and Timucuan words written in the grimoire. Though I didn't understand them, somehow, I knew their meanings.

Whew! It was a lot of work, but when I felt the spell form and radiate from my solar plexus, satisfaction filled me. I could tell the spell was working, and I felt very proud.

Of course, it waited until I was in the shower to alert me about the foreign creature.

❦

WHEN THE SPELL ALERTED ME, it wasn't precise, like a text message. I mean, this spell was devised in the early 1600s. Instead, my "alert" began as a feeling of intense anxiety. Not very helpful, because that's how I feel almost every morning.

As I dried off after my shower, the feeling I was getting shifted to the sensation of danger. It wasn't as if I, personally, was in danger; it was more like the status quo of our ecosystem had been disrupted.

But what was I supposed to do? All I knew was something that didn't belong in Jellyfish Beach had arrived here. I didn't know what it was or where it was.

I opened the grimoire and looked at the spell again. There were no instructions on how to interpret the alert. How was I supposed to enjoy my day off when I had this hanging over me?

And why was I spending my day off searching for a monster, anyway? My life already had vampires, werewolves, ghouls (two houses down from me), and a zombie. I don't need any more monsters. I'm good, thank you. And the Friends of Cryptids Society could wait to add this monster to their database. Sure, there were the Knights Simplar to worry about, but it was difficult to be concerned for the wellbeing of a monster I couldn't even identify.

So, I tried to ignore the bothersome feeling, and it eventually faded to the back burner of my consciousness. I made myself a salad for lunch, topped by a leftover filet from a snapper Matt had caught. After eating, it was time for a well-deserved nap—an indulgence I rarely had time for. I settled on the bed, with the cats eagerly joining me. They loved communal napping. It was even more of a treat when they had me with them.

Sure enough, I was awakened by an uneasy feeling. It was the stupid spell messing with me again.

Bubba meowed when I sat up like I'd been electrocuted. Brenda looked at me as if I was crazy.

This time, the anxiety was more specific and focused. It was about danger, but not to me. The danger was to the monster and others in its vicinity.

I was tired of being teased by this spell. There had to be a way to get more information. All I could think of was to harness some of the energies I had used when creating it and focusing with extra strength on the emotion roiling in my stomach.

It worked. Soon a vague image formed in my mind of the kind of setting where the monster was. This creature wasn't a lone Frankenstein's monster hiding in barns. It was living openly in Jellyfish Beach. The image gained more clarity, becoming like an aerial photo of a community.

A community called Squid Tower.

Then, I received another image. This time, it was the exterior of our botanica. At first, I didn't understand. Why was it showing me two locations?

Because there were two foreign monsters. And my witchy senses gave me the feeling they were of two different species.

Oh, my.

CHAPTER 10
VAMPIRE POLICING COMMITTEE

Right after sunset, my phone rang. Agnes's number appeared on my screen.

"Agnes! Thank heavens you called. Squid Tower is in danger."

"Whatever are you talking about, dear?"

"My familiar told me a new supernatural creature is in town. I performed a magic spell to find the creature and found two of them. One is in your community."

"Vampires are very good at defending our territory," Agnes said in a perfectly calm voice. "No one here has sensed any indication that a dangerous creature is in our midst."

"What about a creature that's not dangerous? Because even if it doesn't harm the residents, it might attract the attention of the Knights Simplar. Then, they would discover that you're all vampires and destroy you."

"My goodness, that sounds terrible. However, I've heard

nothing about any sort of strange creature here. We have pet restrictions, you know."

"I know. Well, please keep your eyes and ears and all your vampire senses attuned to detect any strange creatures that might appear."

"I certainly will."

There had to be something out of the ordinary at Squid Tower. The spell I used was powerful and seemed to have operated properly. The obvious explanation was that the creature was highly skilled at being undetectable.

What if it wasn't a traditional monster? What if it wasn't a critter of some sort but an insect, bacteria, or virus? In that case, it could be very dangerous and difficult to find. I would need to cast an additional spell. Was my magic powerful enough to locate an organism like that?

On the other hand, would such a tiny organism trigger an alert that a supernatural-sensitive entity like Tony would pick up?

I didn't believe the Knights Simplar would care about a strange new virus, even if it came from outer space. And I didn't believe the Friends of Cryptids Society would care, either.

"May I explain now why I called?" Agnes asked. I had almost forgotten she was still on the line.

"I thought I called you."

"No. *I* called to give you important news. We sent a hunting party to look for Heather, Humbert's assistant. They found her."

"Where?"

"In her cottage."

"Did they arrest her?"

"No. She'd been destroyed. Staked. Probably on the night you visited her place and were attacked."

"But that makes no sense."

"We believe she didn't attack you. You were attacked by someone else, who also destroyed Heather."

"Oh, my."

"And I have more news. News you don't want to hear but must. We've arrested your client, Courtney Peppers."

I felt as if the wind had been knocked out of me.

"But why? There's no doubt we were attacked by a vampire."

"You were. Your client is really a vampire."

Whatever wind that hadn't been knocked out of me was gone now. Courtney hadn't seemed like a vampire to me. But, come to think of it, she did meet with us only at night.

"Why would Courtney kill Heather?"

"As Humbert's assistant, Heather would have known many of his secrets. Including the fact that he had turned Courtney. Courtney kept it a secret from you. She couldn't pretend she was human to us, though. Vampires can always identify others of our kind. Her dishonesty with you makes her very suspect in our eyes."

I was surprised I hadn't sensed she was a vampire, especially after all my years of caring for them.

"Still, there are many others who had motives to stake Humbert," I said. "All his fraud victims. Other women he'd turned."

"Courtney could very well have been a fraud victim, too. We don't know yet. Heather would have known. And now, Heather is destroyed."

"I don't know. . ."

"Your client lied to you about being a vampire. She can't be trusted."

"What are you going to do to her?"

"We will continue to interrogate her and investigate. She will be treated fairly."

"And if you decide she's guilty?"

"She will be punished."

"How?"

"Put to the stake."

I gasped audibly.

"Remember," Agnes said, "she's not human. She's one of us, and staking is usually the penalty for vampire murderers."

"Even if the vampire she destroyed was a criminal?"

"The Policing Committee will review mitigating factors before we vote. Perhaps, members will show her mercy."

"What about you?"

"I'm more inclined to show mercy, especially for a vampire so young. The other members might not feel the same way. It has been a long time since one of our residents was murdered."

"Can I speak with her? She's my client, and if you guys don't provide her with a lawyer, I'm all she has."

"Yes, you may speak with her. Be careful, though. She's desperate and could be dangerous."

I HEADED STRAIGHT to Squid Tower. It felt strange driving through Jellyfish Beach, where it was a normal night for all the humans who lived blissfully unaware that vampires existed among them. Passing over the drawbridge onto the barrier island, I entered the land of retirement and beach vacations. Who could imagine a vampire was imprisoned here, with her brief life in so much jeopardy?

Even at Squid Tower, it was hard to imagine. The residents were out enjoying the evening, filling the pickleball and shuffleboard courts. As I walked to the lobby, the swimming pool came into view. It was crowded, as well. I got a quick glimpse of Walt Whitman's naked butt. Obviously, they weren't enforcing the pool rules. They were too busy planning an execution.

My recent magic spell hadn't completely faded yet because I got a jolt of anxiety over the presence of the supernatural entity. As if I didn't already have enough anxiety tonight.

Agnes had told me Courtney was locked up in 305, the rare vacant condo. Despite all the stakings going on, vampires really do enjoy immortality. That means condos rarely become available. Though turning humans is discouraged, it happens, making the vampire population increase even more.

Here in Florida, competition was fierce for homes in vampire-safe communities like this one. Courtney was lucky she wasn't locked up in a storage room.

I was surprised to see Schwartz pulling guard duty outside the door to 305.

"Good evening, Mr. Schwartz. I'm here to see my client, Courtney Peppers."

"Client? You're her nurse?"

"I guess you could say I'm her private investigator."

"I was wondering why your name came up at the Policing Committee meeting."

"I have to admit, I didn't expect you to be a member of the committee. I thought most of the members would be gun-lovers, like Oleg."

"Yes, we got some of them," he said in his heavy Brooklyn accent. "That's why the committee needs some intellectuals, like me. Who else has a brain," he tapped his bald head, fringed with tufts of white hair, "like this one?"

"No one, I'm sure."

"You know, I can't really blame this girl for taking out Humbert. He defrauded so many vampires he probably couldn't keep track of them all."

"Yes, there are lots of people with motives to stake him. More so than the woman you arrested."

"If you don't kill for money, you kill for love. That's what was going on with this young vampire."

"I believe you're mistaken." I wanted to use stronger language than that, but you don't want to get a vampire angry, especially a short-tempered one like Schwartz. "Can I see her now, please?"

He grumbled, fished a key chain from his pocket, grumbled some more, and unlocked the door.

The condo was furnished. Courtney was nowhere in the living areas until I looked up to find her crouching on top of an armoire like a cat.

"Yep, a brand-new vampire," I said. "You haven't yet learned how to resist the feral impulses."

She growled.

"Come down and behave like you're civilized." I took a risk of angering her with my authoritative tone, but I believed it would work.

She jumped down and landed like a gymnast.

"Why didn't you tell us you'd been turned?"

"I was afraid you wouldn't work with me if I did," she said, sitting down on the sofa.

Now that she was composed, she again looked like the woman who had visited our botanica. The woman I'd assumed was human.

"Why not?"

"I figured you would think the conflict between a maker and his child would be beyond your capability to handle. But what I told you was true. I was human when I met him. He mesmerized me, took advantage of me, then turned me."

She was correct that as a human, I couldn't begin to comprehend the dynamics between the two of them. But I understood men who were controlling.

"You wanted to break up with him," I said. "He turned his assistant, too, and she said he dumped her immediately afterward. Why didn't he dump you?"

"He did. I was hoping reverse psychology would work on him, that your asking him to free me would drive him back to me. Especially if the digestive spell worked."

"Why would you want him back?"

"I needed him. After all, he was my maker."

"You weren't honest with us."

"I was honest about his Type O intolerance."

I shook my head in disgust. "Did you stake him?"

"No! Of course not. Why would I hire you if I was going to stake him?"

"Because he wouldn't get back together with you."

"No. I haven't seen him since he brought me back as a vampire."

"Do you have anyone you suspect in his staking?"

"No, I don't. Hugh's world, outside of where I came in, was a mystery to me. He never introduced me to any of his friends."

"I don't believe he had any."

"He said he was semi-retired, but I don't know what kind of work he did, except that it involved financial advising."

"The reason the vampires believe you're guilty is that Mr. Humbert turned you, then abandoned you at your most vulnerable time. It seems he had a history of doing that with other humans he dated. Did he speak of previous women?"

"He did. And I hate it when men do that. But he never admitted turning any of them."

"Did he mention any of them being very upset with him?" I asked, fixing her with my eyes. "If you didn't stake him, I need to find out who did. You're in great danger now of being punished for the crime."

"I know. What gives these vampires the right to lock me up here?"

"They're the self-proclaimed justice system for vampires, since human authorities can't be involved."

"What kind of punishment would they give me?"

"Possibly the ultimate punishment."

Her face grew paler than the deathly white vampire complexion she already had.

"Think hard about what he said regarding his former girl-friends."

"I'm trying to, but now you've got me all panicked. There was a Melissa who tried to call him all the time after he broke up with her. But he never said she was being a psycho or anything."

"Did he mention any jealous boyfriends?"

"No. Well, there was one guy he mentioned. Hugh joked about him. The guy was some dork with a crush on a woman Hugh had been seeing. I don't believe she dated the dork. But he was very jealous of Hugh and told the woman he thought Hugh was a vampire."

"Didn't it concern Mr. Humbert that a human believed he was a vampire?"

"Nah. He said this dork liked to dress up in costumes and claimed to be 'the slayer of evil creatures.' Hugh thought it was so ridiculous he mentioned it to me when he and I first started dating, when I was still awestruck by the fact that vampires really existed."

An unpleasant chill ran down my neck, because this dork sounded like someone I knew all too well.

The self-proclaimed Lord Arseton, commander of the Knights Simplar. This merry band of morons went to Renaissance festivals, fantasy conventions, and anything involving cosplay. They were convinced when people who believe in fantastical creatures got together, they attracted actual fantastical creatures into the world. Creatures the Knights wanted to kill.

Lord Arseton and his thugs somehow realized I was a witch and harassed me until the ghouls who lived on my street ate two of them.

Lord Arseton was a fool, but he was deadly serious about destroying supernatural creatures. He was the last person you'd want to know that vampires existed.

Did he stake Hugh Humbert?

"Did Mr. Humbert mention the guy's name?" I asked.

"No."

I didn't even know Lord Arseton's real name. It could be a coincidence that the dork sounded like him. There are many dorky guys who claim to be monster slayers, right?

The chill on the back of my neck told me this wasn't a coincidence.

"I know of a man who sounds like this dork," I said. "If it's the same person, he could very well be the true murderer of Mr. Humbert. Please try to remember more about the dork and the woman he had a crush on."

"You know it's bad form to talk to your current girlfriend about previous girlfriends. Not that Hugh cared, since he had me mesmerized. Still, he only brought her up in passing."

"If I knew when Mr. Humbert dated her, it would help."

"I think she was right before me. He and I first met in early April."

I needed to get into Humbert's laptop. Hopefully, his calendar would list his social events. If I was lucky, it would have her name. If I was really lucky, his contacts app would have her phone number or email.

"I'm going to look into this," I said, heading for the door. "Keep your spirits up, and I'll return to visit you soon."

"If I haven't been executed by then."

⚰

I ASKED Matt if his friend had made any progress in hacking Humbert's computer. It turned out Sal had already defeated the laptop's security and could operate the machine. The major obstacle so far was gaining access to the clients' financial records. They were presumably inside a financial-planning software platform that had very strong security. He couldn't open the platform to see which clients had suffered unauthorized fund transfers and resulting losses to their accounts.

The laptop's calendar and contacts directory? No problem. Sal reported that in March, right before Humbert began manipulating Courtney, Humbert had four events on weekend evenings with a woman named Lisa. The directory appeared to have clients as well as personal contacts, so it was large. There were four Lisas, two of whom had out-of-state addresses. The other two were local.

Lisa Portnoy was easy to rule out. I called her number to discover she was a state representative who was married with three grandchildren and was the happy recipient of campaign contributions from Humbert.

Lisa Alvarez did not answer her phone. Her voicemail box was full and couldn't accept new messages. An apartment or condo address was included in her listing, so I drove there, hoping for luck.

I found the address, but not the luck.

"Lisa moved out months ago," said the petite woman who had been her roommate. "Moved out sounds too nice. She ghosted me. Went on a date one night with this guy she'd started seeing, and she never came back. She didn't answer her phone, so I called all the hospitals and the police. Finally, she called me one night, said she was okay, and told me she's living somewhere else. Can you believe she left all her things behind?"

"Do you know where she is?" I asked.

"Nope. She refused to tell me, which really hurt my feelings. I think she got into drugs, or something like that. I called her job, and she ghosted them, too."

"Did you meet the guy she went on the date with?"

"Once, briefly. On their second date, he picked her up here. A creepy, older guy named Hugh. I was shocked she would go out with him. They only had like three or four dates before she disappeared."

"What about this guy? Do you know him?"

I had a photo on my phone of Lord Arseton. Like everyone else, his group of goofs had a social-media presence. I found one photo of him in which his head wasn't covered by a costume of some sort.

"Oh, that guy. Can't remember his name. I don't know how she met him, but he pretended to be a friend of hers before declaring he had a thing for her. By then, she had started dating the creepy old guy and told the geek to take a hike."

She didn't have any other useful information for me, so I thanked her and drove home. Along the way, I reviewed what I'd learned.

Based on the behavior Lisa's roommate described, combined with Lisa dating Humbert, I was certain the poor woman had been turned.

And it was no coincidence that the dork who had a crush on her turned out to be Lord Arseton, whatever his real name was. Based on my previous encounter with him, I knew he was a psycho. It was easy imagining him staking Humbert out of jealousy and a misbegotten mission to rid the world of supernatural creatures.

Was he also the one who attacked Matt and me before staking Heather? I couldn't believe a human could move that fast. But if that was the case, it would mean he has already begun tracking down vampires associated with Humbert who might have known Arseton was a bitter rival. Soon, he would discover the vampires living at Squid Tower.

I had to find him quickly.

CHAPTER 11
CRABBY

"Two vampires were staked?" Luisa asked. "That's alarming. You say they suspect our client in both murders?"

She was in the back room, setting up for a Santeria ceremony, placing porcelain bowls containing *Osun* stones on a candle-covered table that served as an altar.

"Yes, they suspect her in both, though, for now, she's only been charged with Humbert's murder."

"I can't believe we couldn't tell when we met with her that she'd already been turned."

"We can't sense who's undead like vampires can, but I should have had a clue. I was their nurse, for Pete's sake. And as a witch, I can sense supernatural beings. But when vampires are recently turned, they retain a lot of human energy at first. They even still have an aura, which takes a while to fade away."

"I thought vampires don't normally stake each other, except for official executions," Luisa said, lighting candles.

"I believe the stakings are a sign of extreme anger and hatred toward the victims. It's not crazy to believe that Courtney did this. She was dating Humbert because he tricked her into thinking he was younger, and then mesmerized her so she would continue to see him. He fed on her against her will and turned her. Then, during her transition, when she needed him the most, he abandoned her."

"Yeah, I'd stab a man to death for a lot less than that," Luisa said.

"The thing is, now there's someone else I suspect."

I told her about how Lord Arseton came into the equation. I'd warned her about him before, because he once showed up at the store to threaten me.

"Do you even know his real name?" she asked.

"No. But I'll find out."

Something bit my ankle. I screamed. The white sheet covering the altar quivered just above the floor.

"Something under the altar bit me!" I said, stepping away from the table. "It must be one of the new monsters."

"New monsters? What are you talking about?"

I explained about the unknown creature Tony had detected and how my spell found two such creatures, one at Squid Tower and one right here in the botanica.

"What bit you is a devil crab," Luisa said.

"You mean *deviled* crab?"

"No. It's a devil crab. It must have remained next door after the seafood takeout place moved out and survived because it has a devil in it."

An open crab claw poked out from the bottom of the sheet, reaching for me.

"It really is a freaking *crab*?" I asked in disbelief.

"It showed up yesterday."

I moved close enough to the altar to lift the edge of the sheet without putting my ankles in harm's way. The crab raised its claws threateningly. Its shell was blue-gray and about six inches wide. Its eye stalks pointed at me in defiance.

"This didn't come from the seafood joint," I said. "They never had live crabs there. This is a blue land crab. He must have wandered into the store from outside."

"Land crab?"

"You're from South Florida, and you've never seen one? Their larvae live in water, but the adults live in burrows that they dig close to the water. The Intracoastal Waterway is only a couple of blocks from here."

"Whatever. This crab has a devil in him."

"I think it's just a regular, cranky—"

I screamed as the crab leaped from the floor and grabbed my nose in its larger pincer. I tried to knock it away without hurting it or my nose. My timid slap did not work.

"Is it possessed by an *orisha*?" I asked desperately.

"Of course not. Orishas are not mean."

"Is it possessed by a voodoo *loa*? I read that Agassu sometimes takes the form of a crab."

"No. It's possessed by a devil."

"Will you help get it off me?"

Bells tinkled above the front door, and in walked two solemn characters, a man and woman, both with jet-black hair and wearing gray suits with gray neckties.

It was Mr. Lopez and Mrs. Lupis from the Friends of Cryptids Society of the Americas.

"Welcome," Luisa said.

"Hey, guys," I said, giving them my biggest fake smile while the land crab dangled from my nose. They always seemed to bring complications to my life.

I had a feeling why they were here today.

"I see you have found one of the new varieties of supernatural creatures in Jellyfish Beach," Mrs. Lupis said.

"You mean this?" I pointed to the crab that was trying to sever my nostril. "It's just a land crab."

"It's a devil crab," said Luisa.

"It's a were-crab," Mr. Lopez said. "Only the second I've ever seen."

"You mean *were*-crab like werewolf?" I asked. My nose was flaring in pain. I considered snapping off the crab's claw, but I had the feeling the Friends of Cryptids would object.

"Yes. It's a rare type of shifter."

"It's rare because shifting involves molting their shells," Mrs. Lupis explained. "It's a very laborious, painful process. When a human shifts into a crab, it could take a year to shift back to human."

"That's horrible," I said.

"That's why were-crabs are even crabbier than real crabs. They are perpetually angry."

"How can I get it off me?" I asked.

"She's female, by the way," Mrs. Lupis said. She approached the crab and whispered something in an unfamiliar language. The creature released my nose, dropped to the floor, and scurried under the altar.

"What did you say?"

"I told her she needs to make an ally of you if she wants to live more comfortably. Your magic will help her shift more smoothly."

I rubbed my throbbing nose, not sure if an angry human would be any better than an angry crab.

"Please record this cryptid in the Society's ledger according to proper procedures," Mr. Lopez said. "We understand there is a second unidentified creature in Jellyfish Beach."

"How did you know this?" I asked.

"Tony tipped us off."

"That little tattletale," I muttered.

"His ability for sensing entities is one reason we gave him to you," Mrs. Lupis said. "He has the sharpest sense of smell of any familiar we've encountered."

"Smell? I thought he sensed the creature through some form of magic or extra-sensory perception."

"He uses all three abilities. But when it comes to scenting, that lizard is as good as a hound dog."

"He uses his tongue like a snake," Mr. Lopez added.

"I cast a spell to identify the community where the other cryptid is. Or was," I said. "But no one there has seen it."

"Where?"

"Squid Tower."

The two exchanged glances.

"This is concerning," Mrs. Lupis said.

"You don't have to tell me. I'm quite aware."

"The world has plenty of vampires," she said, "and they are in no danger of becoming extinct. However, we can't allow their population to be damaged by a predatory creature."

I debated bringing up the danger the Knights Simplar posed to the vampire population, but that topic could wait.

"Do you guys want to search the community?" Luisa asked.

The two solemn characters in suits exchanged glances again.

"That would be ill-advised," Mr. Lopez said.

He didn't explain why. It could be the two were simply afraid of vampires.

The bells tinkled, and all eyes went to the front door. Carl shuffled in wearing his usual funeral suit.

"Hi, Carl," I said.

He moaned in reply and disappeared down an aisle, in search of who knows what.

"Zombie," Mrs. Lupis said.

"We know," Luisa said. "We cataloged him. Carl serves a voodoo priestess we've contracted to provide services to clients. Carl is harmless. As far as I know."

"There has been an increase in zombies in this area," Mr. Lopez said. "Previously, there were only a handful, and most were in a zombie state only temporarily. Now, the most recent census puts their numbers at more than twenty."

"Twenty zombies in Jellyfish Beach? Oh, my." I found this unsettling, even though there have been no problems from the walking dead. As far as I knew.

A heaviness settled into my stomach as I remembered that Lord Arseton had seen Carl during that incident here. Now I worried about Carl's safety as much as the vampires'.

The sound of shoes scraping the floor announced Carl coming out of the aisle, a ceramic statue of a Voodoo loa clasped against his chest. He headed toward the front door.

Luisa rushed over to him. "Hold on, I need to see the price on that."

She blocked Carl's path and attempted to tilt the statuette toward her to read the price sticker on its base.

Carl growled. All of us froze in fear.

But not Luisa. "Come on, be a good zombie. Let me look at the bottom of Papa Legba."

Carl growled louder. He bared his teeth at Luisa, which was easy to do since his lips had mostly rotted away.

"You mind your manners, or I'll take an ax to you!"

Carl whimpered and loosened his grip on the statuette.

"Put twenty dollars on Madame Tibodet's tab, please," Luisa said to me. "Okay, Carl, you can go now."

She stepped out of his way, and he shuffled out the front door, getting into a ride-share car waiting at the curb.

"I can't believe Carl growled at you," I said. "And that you didn't run away."

"Oh, he's harmless. It's like your dog growling when you pull his chew toy from his mouth."

"Zombies view humans as chew toys."

"Please tell your priestess to keep her zombie under control," Mrs. Lupis said. "We can't afford to have a zombie uprising. Now, back to the main topic."

"Yes." Mr. Lopez fixed me with a commanding stare. "We originally sought you out because of your expertise with vampires and werewolves."

"And trolls, ogres, and other creatures," Mrs. Lupis added.

"We're depending on you to search Squid Tower."

"And determine what this creature or organism is."

"Perhaps, it's not a predator, but more of a parasite," I suggested. "Or it has a symbiotic relationship with the vampires."

"We await your findings," said Mrs. Lupis.

I wasn't eager to get involved, but the Society basically owned Luisa and me.

"I'll do my best," I said, adding it to my list of to-dos. Exonerating my client was at the top. But I also needed to protect the vampires from a creature potentially more dangerous than an unidentified cryptid.

◦◦◦◦◦◦

I HAD GIVEN up on using the internet to search for Lord Arseton's identity. The Knights Simplar and the name Lord Arseton occasionally appeared on the fringes of the web, but never with the actual names of people. I didn't just use search engines; I also searched the online archives of *The Jellyfish Beach Journal* and other publications. Still, I came up short.

When he had confronted me at the botanica, Lord Arseton mentioned his real job was repairing smartphones. So, I cased out the various retail establishments that provided this service. I hoped he wasn't some independent contractor who worked from home, because I would need to see his face to recognize him. And I couldn't allow him to see mine. Therefore, I couldn't simply walk into a store looking for him. I had to park outside each store before it opened, hoping to see him arrive for work.

I spent days checking out all the stores of the major cellular carriers that did minor repairs onsite. I had no luck.

Next, I tried independent repair stores. One morning, I was parked at a seedy strip mall facing a shop called, "You Break It,

We Try to Fix It." A dorky guy in a hoodie walked past my car and unlocked the shop's door.

It was Lord Arseton.

Now was not the time to confront him. I needed to gather information and clues first. Going to the website of the store, I found the name of the manager, Tim Tissy. Given that the only other employee who showed up at the store was a young man barely out of his teens, it seemed safe to assume that Arseton was the manager. And therefore, he was Tim Tissy.

I searched the Property Appraiser's website and found a condo owned by Tissy and jotted down the address. A search of public records netted a lawsuit that seemed unrelated and— wait, here was a restraining order to stay away from Lisa Alvarez.

Okay, I was finally getting somewhere. Tissy was the unsuccessful suitor of Lisa and behaved in such a way that she needed to file a restraining order against him. That marked the kind of irrational, angry man who would gladly stake the vampire who had stolen his love interest.

But could I prove he staked Humbert? Nope. And to prove he also staked Heather because she somehow knew about his crime would be even more difficult.

The only thing I could think to do at this point was to tail him and learn about his activities.

That required taking at least one day off from work. Luisa was not happy when I called her.

"Let's just cut Courtney loose," she said. "Courtney concealed from us that she's a vampire, and the vampires at Squid Tower think she's guilty. You've already spent too much time on this."

"I think she's innocent," I said. "Maybe it's just a gut feeling, but I can't abandon her and allow her to be executed."

"She's a vampire. They're predatory monsters in my book."

"And we're supposed to protect them, according to the folks who bankrolled us. Besides, I think a human might be the murderer."

"Who?"

"Lord Arseton. The guy who thinks I should die because I'm a witch."

"Oh, that guy. What a jerk."

"I want to put him away."

"Okay, okay. Keep playing detective if you insist. Just don't come crying to me when it gives you a nervous breakdown."

"I wouldn't come crying to you under any circumstances."

"Good. And you'd better show up at the botanica tomorrow."

"Okay. Thanks for giving me some slack."

So, I sat in the strip-mall parking lot, waiting for Tissy to go to lunch. When he finally came out of the store at midday, he went to a place that sold video games before returning to the store. I realized it was a waste of time to surveil him while he was at work, so I drove to the botanica to put in some hours, making Luisa much happier.

The phone repair shop closed at 7:00 p.m., so I parked nearby shortly before that time. When Tissy locked up behind him and his employee, I followed his car. I'd never tried to tail anyone before, but he didn't appear to suspect anyone would, so I didn't have to be too careful.

I wouldn't find evidence that Tissy had staked the vampires simply by following him. Only by breaking into his condo might I find clues. My main reason for following him was to make sure he wasn't surveilling Squid Tower.

He ended up at a sad-looking, two-story condo complex outside of town at the same address as the Property Appraiser's listing. He parked and entered his condo. I made note of the unit's location should I decide to break in. Then, I waited, not knowing if he would come out again.

About an hour later, he did, causing my adrenaline to flow. I slumped down in the seat, hoping he wouldn't see me. After he pulled onto the street, I started my car and caught up with him.

Fortunately, he didn't drive to Squid Tower. No, he drove to my house.

While I was surveilling him, he was doing the same to me.

He parked two houses away from mine. I didn't believe he would recognize my car, but just in case, I parked two houses behind him.

I waited for him to do something. He waited for me. I supposed he was looking for monsters entering or leaving my home. Eventually, he realized I wasn't home and drove away.

I felt violated having this creep stalking me at my home. My hands shook slightly. Was it from rage or fear?

CHAPTER 12
CREATURE HUNTING

I decided to keep following Lord Arseton, whom I simply couldn't bring myself to call by his real name. He was a fool living a delusion, so I might as well think of him by his imaginary name.

It was dark now, so I waited a few moments to avoid alarming him with my headlights instantly appearing in his rearview mirror. Once we were out of my neighborhood, I pulled a little closer behind his car. He still drove as if he didn't know he was being tailed.

He turned right onto Jellyfish Beach Boulevard, and two blocks later, turned left onto Third Avenue. When he turned onto Sixth Street, I knew where he was going.

The botanica.

The shop was still open, with all its lights blazing, but would close soon. Arseton parked across the street and turned off his headlights. I figured he was hoping to see monsters come out of the shop. Instead, a heavyset older woman waddled out holding a plastic bag of her purchases. She didn't look like a monster to me.

Soon afterward, the lights in the shop went out, and Luisa emerged. After locking the front door and closing the metal shutters, she got into her car, which sat in the small parking lot out front, and drove away.

Lord Arseton followed her, and I followed him. Luisa had no idea she was leading an entire procession.

The route to Luisa's house was short. She parked in her driveway next to her elder daughter's car. There were other cars parked along the curb, so Arseton's and mine stood out less when we parked near them.

Luisa went inside. She was a single mother with two daughters. One was twenty, and the other was sixteen. The thought of Arseton stalking this family made me increasingly angry as I sat in my dark car.

I understood his obsession with me, as silly as it was. I was a witch, born with genes that gave me the natural ability to create magic. Not being a normal human, I was a target of Arseton's quasi-religious crusade against fantastical creatures.

Luisa, however, was a normal human. Yes, she was a Santeria priestess, and if Arseton had a problem with that, it was because of his own prejudice. As far as I was concerned, Luisa was like any member of the clergy of other religions.

Moreover, she didn't have a ghost and a talking iguana in her home like I did. Nor did she associate with vampires, werewolves, trolls, and other strange creatures. She was a typical working-class person trying to get by.

I could text Luisa, explain the situation, and tell her to call the cops on this stalker. This dude already had a restraining order against him for stalking another woman.

But he needed more persuasion than a police officer telling him to move on.

I got out and walked across the street to Arseton's vehicle. The glow of his phone's screen illuminated his face as he stared at a video game.

I rapped my knuckles on his window. He jumped in surprise.

When he rolled down the window, I said, "Leave this family alone, you weirdo."

"I don't know what you're talking about," he said, his hackles rising. "I'm minding my own business, and I suggest you mind yours."

"You're stalking a single mother and her children. That's sick."

"She sells supplies for satanic rituals and worships heathen gods. She—and you—are the ones who are sick."

"Speaking of sick, I know all about you, creep. Your name is Tim Tissy, and you have at least one restraining order against you. I'm going to file for another one."

"Don't you threaten me, witch." Spittle sprayed with his words. He was so demonically angry, I half expected his head to rotate 360 degrees.

"You murdered two people by driving stakes through their hearts, and you will be punished for it."

I didn't mention that his victims were vampires because I didn't want to validate his belief in them.

"I don't know what you're talking about," he said. "But your foul, evil, witch's heart deserves a stake in it."

"Leave me, Luisa, and the botanica alone. Stick with dressing up in costumes."

During our exchange, I had been building and gathering my energies. Reciting the words of my spell under my breath, I sent the magic directly to its target.

His bowels. It was my patented laxative spell. It was so effective I could make millions selling it to gastroenterologists to give to their patients for colonoscopy prep. If only doctors believed in magic.

Arseton looked confused. His expression quickly turned to distress.

"I have to go home," he said, starting his car. "Watch your back, witch, because I'm . . . oh, no!"

His tires squealed as he sped off down the street.

I wondered if he'd make it home in time.

KNOWING for certain that Arseton couldn't follow me, I drove to Squid Tower to check on my vampire friends. I was worried about the unidentified creature allegedly in their midst.

When I got out of my car, I felt none of the anxiety I had when I was still under the influence of my creature-hunting spell. My witchy senses picked up plenty of supernatural energies, but that was typical in a community of vampires.

It was a normal early evening there. The Blood Bus was parked near the front entrance, and a long line of residents formed at its window where the employees were handing out pint bags of blood.

As I headed toward the lobby, I glanced through the open breezeway to the pool area, and a flickering light caught my eyes. There appeared to be a bonfire on the beach.

This was abnormal for Squid Tower. Could a group of humans be there? It wasn't the wisest place for them to have a bonfire.

After walking along the boardwalk to the dune crossover, I saw elderly vampires sitting cross-legged on the beach around the fire, gazing up at Walt Whitman. He stood on the steps to the beach below me, reciting poetry.

I recognized the words from "Song of Myself." It was a lengthy poem, and he was only partway through it. As I looked more closely at his audience, I realized half of them were asleep, their heads resting on their chests. Several others were fighting the urge to nod off. It was unlikely they would be so tired this early in the evening, but that's what long-form poetry can do to you if it's not your thing.

I turned away before I got sleepy myself and headed to the tower to visit Agnes. Walking through the lobby, I cleared my mind and opened my witchy senses, trying to feel if the supernatural energy increased. Like a Geiger counter measuring radiation, I hoped I would pick up an increase in supernatural energy if I got closer to the mysterious creature.

I felt no change and took the elevator to Agnes's floor. She didn't answer her door. I decided to wander around the community to look for her and see if the supernatural energy increased while I was at it.

I already knew she wasn't at the bonfire poetry reading. She wasn't in the community room. Nor was she in the card room, where a group of vampires has spent the last fourteen years attempting to complete a diabolically difficult jigsaw puzzle. Vampires have unlimited patience, born from their immortality.

Nor was Agnes in the lounge, where two vampires played Ping-Pong. It was no fun for a human to watch vampires play a Ping-Pong match. The players and the ball moved too quickly for the human eye to register. And every few minutes, the game would be interrupted after the ball was crushed by excessive force.

Being a vampire was not all about drinking blood. It was about finding ways to entertain yourself for eternity.

Next, I went outside in search of Agnes or a spike in supernatural energies. So far, I'd found neither.

Agnes had no interest in pickleball, so I skipped the courts. She wasn't playing shuffleboard tonight and wasn't in the swimming pool or hot tubs.

I didn't head toward the horseshoe pit until I heard the *thunk* of objects striking wood.

A bunch of vampires were gathered, but they weren't watching the tossing of horseshoes at a metal rod in the round. A plywood target had been erected behind the rod.

And Agnes was throwing spears, with great accuracy, at the target.

Mind you, Agnes had a body age of around ninety years old. Having been raised by a Visigoth warrior in the twilight of the Roman Empire, Agnes knew how to throw a spear. But to watch the diminutive nonagenarian fling the weapon with such accuracy and force that the steel spearhead popped out on the backside of the target was awe-inspiring.

Even allowing for the extra vampire strength, this was amazing.

I gave her enthusiastic applause.

The vampires looked at me with amusement. Beatrice, Henrietta, Sol, Oleg, and Gladys were the audience. Agnes walked toward me with a huge grin.

"Want to give it a try?" she asked.

"I've never thrown a spear in all my life. And I was horrible at archery in summer camp."

"Back in my day, that meant you'd be relegated to cooking, weaving, and child-rearing. But you have a warrior's heart, my dear."

"Right now, I've declared war on whatever unusual supernatural entity is here at Squid Tower."

"You still believe one is here?"

"Yes. And so does my familiar. Have you seen no signs of one?"

"I have not," Agnes said. "And I've heard no reports of any sightings."

"Has there been anything out of the ordinary? Strange odors or sounds? Residents acting odd? You know, this creature could be in any form, even a microorganism."

"I can't think of anything. Well, there does seem to be a general malaise among some of us lately, but I've chalked that up to seasonal affective disorder, with the nights being so short this time of year."

"Okay." I was frustrated by getting no results. Perhaps, Tony had simply been wrong. "I also came here tonight to tell you I'm making progress in finding Humbert's actual murderer. I suspect a certain human."

My phone buzzed with a text. It was from Matt announcing his friend had hacked his way into Humbert's financial-planning software. They would drop the laptop off at my home tonight, so I could search the database for clients who had lost large amounts of money.

"Sorry," I said to Agnes. "I have to meet a friend of Matt's at my house. He was able to hack into Humbert's laptop. But financial losses clearly weren't the motive. I believe this human did it out of jealousy over a woman Humbert was dating and then turned. This human is a fanatic. He leads that cult I told you about that is on a mission to destroy supernatural creatures."

"He knows vampires exist? How disturbing."

"Yes. Please delay the trial of my client while I search for more evidence. I believe I'll convince you that this human is the murderer."

"I hope you're correct."

"And please send word to the residents to watch out for any humans loitering near the property."

"My, you're quite the taskmaster. We must hunt for an unknown supernatural creature *and* a psychotic human."

"Of the two, the human is probably more dangerous."

⸎

When I arrived home, I fed Brenda and Bubba, who were decidedly not happy about my late arrival. If they understood English, they would realize I had a good excuse. I checked on Tony in the garage. He was already asleep. I replenished his water plus his bowl of lettuce and mixed fruit, but Tony's preferred meals were flowers foraged from my neighbors' gardens. They were not happy about that.

I checked my stock of beer in the fridge right before the doorbell rang.

Matt stood on the front porch with a hulking guy who was as far from the stereotype of a computer nerd as you could be.

"Missy," Matt said, "this is Sal."

"Great to meet you. Thanks so much for your help," I said to the man with the shaved head and the build of a pro-football player.

I gave beers to the two men, made tea for myself, and joined them already at the kitchen table.

"The financial-planning software was a beast to hack into," Sal said, opening the laptop. His fingers seemed too beefy to type effectively, but they were quite nimble as he brought up the home screen. He handed me a slip of paper. "Here's the guy's username and the new password."

"Thank you so much. Um, so what am I supposed to do?"

"You'll need to spend time exploring and familiarizing yourself with the interface. But this menu here leads you to a list of his clients. Click on a name, and it will take you to their individual home page. It gets kind of complicated with all the charts and graphs, but you can see their gains and losses. You're looking for people who lost a lot of money?"

"Yes," I replied. "Especially losses because of fraud."

"You might need an accountant to help you recognize fraud."

"I can help you," Matt said. "I've investigated plenty of fraudsters and know some signs to look for."

"Hm, that's strange," Sal said. "This account here says it was opened almost two hundred years ago. Must have been a typo during the data entry."

I couldn't explain to him that the year was probably accurate, and the account was previously recorded with pen and ink on paper.

Matt gave me an ironic smile. He knew what I was thinking.

"Sal," I said. "I can't thank you enough. I insist you accept—"

The kitchen window imploded as a masked, black-clad figure shot inside.

It looked like a ninja but growled like a vampire. With a single swing of its arm, it sent Sal flying backward, landing on the floor, and slamming his head into the refrigerator. As Matt and I leaped to our feet, the creature grabbed Matt and threw him over the island counter.

I backed away and frantically cast a simple protection spell for myself to prevent the creature from knocking me out or killing me. Then, I would use a warding spell to get it out of my house.

But the creature wasn't interested in me. It grabbed the laptop, dashed to the broken window, and leaped out.

The attack had lasted mere seconds. In that brief moment, I couldn't tell if the creature was male or female. It was of medium build and could have been either gender. Its face was covered with a ski mask, and it moved too quickly. But speculation had to wait. I had two injured patients to care for.

Fortunately, both were conscious, though Matt was groaning. A little too dramatically, in my opinion. He was on the floor on the other side of the island, tangled in a fallen bar stool. He got to his feet.

I crouched to look at Sal. He was sitting upright, looking stunned, but not in pain.

"Are you okay?" I asked, searching his eyes for signs of a concussion. "How does your head feel?"

"Fine. When I hit the floor, my back took the brunt of it."

"I meant when your head hit the fridge." I pointed out the large dent in the stainless steel.

"Oh, sorry about that."

"Don't apologize."

"Who the heck attacked us? Man, they took the laptop."

"It was a ninja," I said. "My neighborhood has been experiencing a ninja crime spree lately."

"I guess too many ninjas are out of work," Matt said.

"Yeah. I wish the politicians would do something about it. Anyway, as I was about to say when I was rudely interrupted, I want to pay you for your services, Sal. And don't argue with me. You just took a header into my fridge for me."

"Sorry I dented it."

"Blame the ninja."

Sal tried to refuse payment, but I stuffed a wad of bills in his hand, gave him a homemade muffin, and sent him on his way.

"The ninja was a vampire, wasn't it?" Matt asked.

"Of course. You haven't heard any reports of ninja burglars in Jellyfish Beach, have you?"

"I can't believe how terrible the timing was. You finally got tons of data at your fingertips and didn't have time to look at a single client record."

"You don't need to remind me. I told Agnes just this evening that I was going to get into the records."

"That wasn't Agnes, was it?"

"I refuse to believe it. I wonder if she told this vampire about the laptop. But why would she do that?"

Matt popped open another beer without asking. While he was taking a swig, I told him about Lord Arseton's actual identity of Timothy Tissy.

"If this ninja was a vampire, it derails your theory about him, doesn't it?" he asked.

"Maybe, maybe not. The only thing we can be certain of is that the vampire thief had information on the laptop he or she didn't want us to see."

"Yeah, like they were defrauded by Humbert."

"Or it could be something about their private life."

"Like nude pictures?"

"Gross." I thought about it for a moment. "Well, I guess there could be something like that. Old Humbert was quite a randy old vampire."

"Aside from any naughty photos, that computer had very valuable data on it," Matt said. "Humbert must have backed it up, either in the cloud or on an external drive."

"Yeah. If Sal is still talking to us, can you ask him if he can access Humbert's account in the cloud somehow?"

"Yeah, I'll ask him. You should get access to Humbert's condo to search for an external hard drive."

"I will. If the ninja hasn't stolen it already. In the meantime, I'm going to keep looking into Arseton. That guy is one dangerous dweeb."

CHAPTER 13

THE ANGEL MYRON

I didn't believe Arseton had seen my car when I confronted him. Even if he had, he probably wouldn't remember. My ride looked like the kind of vehicle that someone buys used from someone else who bought it used. Except, I'd owned it since the beginning of my nursing career.

So, I began tailing Arseton again. I honestly believed he had a stronger motive for committing the stakings than some vampire who lost money or had nudes on an ex-boyfriend's computer. Arseton was a nut who obsessed over a woman he couldn't have, thanks to Humbert.

The major flaw in my reasoning was the unlikelihood that Arseton had the speed and strength of the creature that attacked us at Heather's home and at mine.

But I was blinded by my hatred of Arseton. I prefer to see myself as a good person who is above hating. But not in Arseton's case. After all, the dude thinks I should be burned because I'm a witch.

I sat in my car in the strip-mall parking lot until Arseton and his employee closed the store. My quarry drove to a fast-food restaurant and took the bag to his apartment. I found a parking spot where a large Banyan tree blocked the light from the streetlamps, its roots cracking the asphalt beside it.

An hour passed as I sat, engine off, windows cracked open, listening for any sounds of trouble. For all I knew, Arseton would stay in all night. I wondered how he entertained himself at home—whether he read, watched TV, or just played games on his phone. All I knew was that the subject matter would be weird.

His front door on the second floor opened, and he came out carrying a garment bag—probably a costume of some sort.

He descended the exterior stairs and got into his car, which wasn't much newer than mine. I waited for him to drive past me before I started my engine and followed him. It was early enough in the evening that there was still a fair amount of traffic, so it was easy to follow him without worrying about being discovered.

He traveled south on the interstate to the next city. When he exited, he turned east, and I expected him to continue into the downtown area, but instead, he made an abrupt turn into a hotel overlooking the highway. I parked next to an RV and watched Arseton walk into the hotel with his garment bag. Other men and women arrived carrying similar garment bags.

Was this a meeting of fans dressing up as Star Trek or Star Wars characters? Or was it a religious cult? I really wanted to find out. And, as a witch, I had a way to do it that didn't involve crashing the party and being thrown out.

First, I entered the hotel and walked through the lobby as if

I knew where I was going, looking for where the meeting rooms were. They were on the ground floor at the north end of the building. A geeky man carrying a garment bag disappeared into a room called the Starfish. A cardboard sign on an easel said, "Private."

Next, I went outside and walked around the building to the north side. Placing my hands against the brick wall outside of the meeting room, I gathered my energies. I then created a bond with the earth energy of the brick, the concrete blocks behind it, and the drywall on the interior side. I would attract attention if I stood here for too long with my hands on the wall. That's why I made a psychic connection with it, as if I were attaching physical wires. Now, I could return to my car and create the spell.

It was a basic penetration spell, allowing my energy to pass through the wall at a molecular level, seeping through the building materials like water through sand. Though it wasn't a complicated spell, it required a great deal of energy to perform, and only a highly experienced witch could pull it off. I grasped a power charm to amplify my energies while I recited the incantation.

Soon, muffled voices appeared in my head, along with a blurry image of a room filled with people. These sensory inputs gradually sharpened until it was as if I were in the room myself.

No, it was not a meeting of the Star Trek Fan Club. It appeared to be a religious meeting. Although, not of any religion that I knew.

Men and women in their twenties to fifties, overwhelmingly Caucasian, wore white tunics with an embroidered eyeball on the front. They stood in a large circle, holding hands, surrounding Arseton in the center. Everyone's eyes were closed except for his. He chanted in a deep, overly dramatic voice like a voiceover in a car-dealer commercial.

"We must step up our battle against the perversions walking among us. The monsters born of Satan. In our very own Jellyfish Beach, there are witches and zombies! Yes, I have seen them. We must slay them!"

"Slay them!" the congregation echoed in unison.

"There are vampires! Yes, for I have witnessed them," Arseton chanted.

"Slay them!"

"There are werewolves!"

"Slay them!"

"There are alien lizard people who run the world!"

"Slay them!"

"There are secret cabals that plot against us!"

"Slay them!"

"There are people I disagree with!"

"Slay them!"

"There are men who wear their baseball caps crooked."

"Slay them!"

One guy looked up nervously.

"There are the wicked movie makers who peddle smut."

"Slay them!"

"And all the perverted people who watch their smut!"

Four people looked up nervously.

"Slay them!"

"There are coffeeshop owners who charge seven bucks for a pumpkin-spice Frappuccino!"

"Slay them!" the crowd roared with ferocity.

"There are the wicked motorists who miss the light turning green because they're playing with their phones."

No response.

"Well?" Arseton demanded.

"Slay them!"

"There's the person who invented corn dogs."

"Slay him!"

"Wait," one guy muttered. "What's wrong with corn dogs?"

"Slay him!"

Two men broke away from the circle and dragged the corn-dog defender from the room.

"There are mosquitoes. Way too many mosquitoes."

"Slay them!"

"Lima beans!"

"Slay them?"

"All these people and things have something in common," Arseton continued. "They're not just what *I* hate—and there are a lot more people and things I hate, by the way. They're all part of a secret global conspiracy."

"Even the mosquitoes and lima beans?" a brave congregant asked.

"Especially the mosquitoes! They hate us even more than I hate them. And they want to destroy America! Not the mosquitoes, but all the others I mentioned."

"Slay them!"

"I know this for a fact because the Angel Myron appeared before me and told me. He said hatred is good, and it strengthens us. And when we eliminate all things we hate, we will be stronger. Glory be to Myron."

"Glory be," they all responded.

"I pray for the Angel Myron to grace us with his presence if we are worthy. Come to us, Myron."

"Come to us, Myron."

The sensory input from my magic dimmed. I worried that the spell was fading, or some external force was interfering. Suddenly, the acuity returned.

And a glowing eye was floating above the circle of worshippers. It was a sphere about the size of a basketball, looking exactly like an eyeball but without the ugly veins. It was white with a black pupil and yellow iris, just like the image embroidered on the tunics everyone wore.

The circle of congregants knelt. Arseton remained standing, his arms raised toward the orb floating just above.

Sorry, but this eyeball didn't look like an angel to me. It looked like a demon. And I've encountered demons before, so I know what I'm talking about. Besides, Mrs. Lupis and Mr. Lopez had told me the Knights Simplar were under the influence of a demon. This eyeball named Myron must be the one.

The question was, how did they find the demon—or how did it find them? Summoning a demon required black magic and was difficult. My mother was one of the few people I knew who could do it.

Please don't tell me my mother was involved with this.

A short, bald man walked into the room. He gasped when he saw the hovering eyeball, and his face turned red when everyone turned to stare at him.

"Sorry. I thought this was the Kiwanis Club meeting."

"Sandpiper Room, next door," Arseton said.

Some small, non-traditional churches rent whatever spaces they can get. But you would think if you're going to summon a demon, you would pick a place other than a hotel meeting room. But that's just me.

Myron, the angel who was probably a demon, disappeared. Arseton quickly recited what sounded like a concluding prayer to end the ceremony.

I broke the penetration spell and sat in my car, feeling confounded. This strange cult that I first met at a Renaissance festival, with dudes wearing suits of chain mail and pretending to be knights, was more dangerous than I had thought. Arseton was still a clown in my eyes, but having the ability to summon a demon could mean he was a sorcerer, too.

Unless the demon showed up of its own free will. Maybe it was the demon pulling the strings and not Arseton.

I couldn't decide which scenario was worse.

⸎

"Man, a cult right here in Jellyfish Beach?" Matt asked over the phone. His voice sounded like I'd just given him a gift. "I've heard nothing about these guys. Are they part of the Knights Simplar, or totally separate?"

"How would I know? I only followed him to the hotel and cast a penetration spell."

"I've got to find out more about this."

"The journalism gears are turning in your head, but you understand you can't report about the demon," I said.

Matt and I had long ago agreed that I would give him inside knowledge of the supernatural world if he agreed not to reveal it to the public. The pact of secrecy was inviolable when humans dealt with supernaturals. Furthermore, he realized that publishing this kind of thing would discredit him as a serious journalist. He might make good money selling such stories at first. However, he would be pushed aside into the fringes of the internet, or his stories would mainstream the supernatural and no longer be exclusive to him.

"I could write about a demon-worshipping cult without stating that there really is a demon," he said.

"I find the whole affair filled with contradictions. When we first encountered Arseton, I thought he was the typical religious fanatic who wanted to kill witches and supernatural entities because he considered them unholy. But now, he has all these other targets of his hate. Like lima beans. And how can you be a soldier of God when you're worshipping a demon? Even if he calls it an angel."

"I think you answered your own question. He might truly believe the demon is an angel. Arseton is a self-appointed warrior against evil. He meets an angel—which he believes is evidence of his righteousness—but the quote-unquote angel steers him in a most unholy direction without his realizing it."

"Yeah, Arseton is not exactly self-aware," I said.

"And for the record, I hate lima beans, too."

"I guess that makes you righteous."

"I need to infiltrate this group."

"Look, my mission is to find out if Arseton staked the vampires and if he knows about the others living in Jellyfish Beach. I don't want to go down a rabbit hole with this cult."

"Well, I do."

"Have yourself a good time. But you'd better not let Arseton know that I've found out about the cult."

CHAPTER 14
GOING UNDERCOVER

It was like putting a wire on a secret informant. Except in this circumstance, I was attaching my surveillance spell to Matt. I used a lock of his hair in a complex mixture of herbs and minerals, imbued it with magic, and placed the enchanted potpourri in a small cloth sack. This amulet would connect me with Matt and allow me to share his sensory input.

"Wow, this feels pretty intimate," Matt said as he hung the cord attached to the amulet around his neck and placed the cloth sack under his shirt. "And you and I haven't been, you know, intimate yet."

"Remember, you're the one who turned down my offer."

"Yes, and remember, I said I wanted to be in your heart—not just your bed."

Connecting the surveillance spell to Matt this way was much more effective and powerful than when I had penetrated the wall before. It brought my spell directly into the room, rather than boring through concrete and drywall. Plus, I would maintain a connection to Matt wherever he went, should something happen to him.

The spell was the best part of our plan. Getting Matt into the hotel meeting room was the weak part. We had tried but couldn't find a way to contact the cult so that Matt could apply for membership. He found a social-media page for the Knights Simplar, but it was invitation-only.

Instead, Matt was simply going to bluff his way into the next ceremony. Based on my memories, I found a white tunic like the ones the congregation had worn and had it embroidered with an eye symbol that was as close as possible to the one on theirs.

Since there were more than twenty members, Matt hoped he could just show up and blend in. I wasn't so sure. But if anyone could talk his way out of trouble, it was Matt.

I drove him to the hotel at the same time and on the same night of the week Arseton had gone there before, hoping it was a weekly event. Sure enough, people were streaming into the lobby, carrying garment bags.

"Wish me luck," Matt said, leaning in to give me a quick kiss. Before I could say anything, he was out of the car and striding briskly into the hotel.

I parked on an outer edge of the parking lot, away from all traffic, where I could concentrate. I chanted the words that activated the spell that connected me with Matt's charm. It was like a psychic wireless connection.

I cleared my mind and sent forth my energies. Then, I waited.

At first, the sounds and images were blurry and muddy. But soon, I was in a stall in the men's room, taking the tunic from the garment bag and pulling it over my clothes. When I say "I," I mean Matt. It was as if we were one and the same.

"Hey, buddy. Are you new?" asked the overweight man who popped out of the adjoining stall.

"Uh, yeah," Matt/I said. Anxiety surged inside us.

"Who recruited you?"

"Um, Timothy."

"Who?"

"Lord Arseton."

"His Holiness himself! Well, I hope you have an experience as moving as I've had. I feel like I have a purpose now. There's nothing like hatred to put meaning in your life."

"I'll say."

"I'm Bob, owner of Bob's Appliances."

"I'm Matt. I'm, um, a musician."

"Cool. Maybe you can perform for us sometime. The annual potluck supper and rummage sale is coming up."

"Sounds like fun," Matt said. "Should we go in now?"

Matt followed Bob into the Starfish Room. A group of Shriners in tubular hats was filing into the room next door. Everyone needs activities outside of work, though most don't involve demons.

Entering the meeting room, Matt found the congregation already forming a circle. Matt took Bob's beefy hand in his left, and the soft hand of an attractive woman in his right.

Man, she's hot, Matt thought.

Stop it! I thought back, though I wasn't sure if my thoughts traveled in the opposite direction to him.

A few of the people on the other side of the circle looked at

Matt curiously. He smiled and nodded, trying to exude the feeling that he belonged here.

When Arseton entered the room, the crowd went silent. He wasn't the type of faith leader who greeted his followers personally; he played the role of a messianic figure who was above them. They seemed to like this and gazed at him with adoration.

Two women released their hands to allow Arseton to enter the circle.

"Let us pray, my brethren. In the name of the Angel Myron, we denounce our enemies and vow to destroy them."

The crowd repeated his words. Matt felt both silly and uneasy at the same time.

"My brethren, we nurture the hatred in our hearts, and it gives us strength," Arseton said. "Yet, nurturing it is not enough. It soon becomes meaningless unless we act upon it. Let hatred in action be our motto."

"Hatred in action!" the crowd replied, though not in unison.

"We must do more than hate our enemies. We must slay them!"

"Slay them," the congregation chanted. They'd had a lot of practice with this chant.

"Make them suffer, and then wipe them off the face of this earth so that they do not trouble our vision any longer. We must slay them!"

"Slay them!"

"It is time that we carry out this vow. Hatred in Action."

"Hatred in Action!"

"I have assembled a list of those we hate who will suffer our wrath. I shall select the first target."

"My neighbor, Izzy!" shouted Bob.

Arseton glared at him. "I do not take requests."

After scolding Bob, he noticed Matt and stared at him suspiciously for a moment. Matt's insides turned to ice.

"Now, where was I?"

"You were telling us who we're going to slay," offered the woman to Matt's right.

"Yes. There are so many people I hate who are all wicked," Arseton continued. "However, we will begin by slaying actual monsters. There are legions of these fiends from Hell living among us in Jellyfish Beach. The Angel Myron has decreed that we shall slay them without delay. We begin tonight. I need four volunteers to assist me—men in decent physical condition."

Most of the congregation were men, and they all raised their hands except for Matt. Realizing this made him stand out, he raised his hand, too.

Arseton pointed to three of the younger, more fit men, skipped Bob, then pointed at Matt.

"And you, New Guy. Keep your tunics on and follow me. I have a rental van parked in the back."

I felt Matt's fear and consternation, but I was happy he was selected. It was the only way I would know where Arseton was going and whom he intended to "slay."

A white van rolled around from the rear of the hotel. I texted Agnes, warning her to put the community on alert and watch out for a white van. Then, I started my car and followed the van into the night.

All this activity disrupted my connection to Matt's amulet and, thus, to his senses. The spell was still working, though. I'd had to put it on pause while I concentrated on my own senses for driving.

The van wasn't going to Squid Tower as I had feared, nor was it headed toward my home or Luisa's so they could slay one of us. I assumed, then, it was headed to a vampire nest I wasn't aware of.

We were now on the outskirts of town in a neighborhood I wasn't very familiar with. It was a working-class community where many Haitian immigrants had settled over the years.

The van entered a side street and turned off its lights, though it still moved forward. I did the same. The van pulled over to the curb and parked near a ranch-style home with candles in the windows, gaily painted in tropical colors. I parked two houses behind the van.

With my car turned off, I tuned out the world around me and focused my energies on the spell. My face tingled as my magic returned to the forefront. Soon, my connection to Matt was restored as he climbed from the back of the van. He/I reluctantly followed the others through the freshly mown lawn into the backyard of the targeted house.

The yard was filled with vegetable gardens. In a corner, beneath a large mango tree, was a shed with tiny windows. Arseton went straight to the shed. For the first time, Matt noticed the man carried a crowbar, which he immediately used to pry the hasp of a latch sealed with a padlock. Using violent wrenching motions, Arseton popped the hasp and its screws from the wood of the door.

"The creature is uncoordinated, but strong and violent," he

whispered to his acolytes. "We will use our numbers to restrain him, then tie him with this rope."

He handed a coil of rope to the man in front of Matt. The men looked at each other nervously.

Arseton yanked the shed door open.

Though their leader had been acting theatrically bold this evening, he wasn't the first one to enter the shed. No, he stood aside, behind the opened door, and gestured for the others to go inside.

Matt made only one step into the hot dark space that reeked of incense and rotting flesh. Something deep in the darkness growled, one of the men squealed, and the guy in front of Matt fell backward, knocking Matt off balance and onto his butt in the grass. The shed swayed from the impact of bodies hitting the walls.

Matt forced himself to go back into the shed, just as the others were coming out, holding another man wrapped in ropes. The captured man wore a business suit, and his face was badly decomposed.

Matt recognized him. So did I. The prisoner was Carl the Zombie.

I should have expected Carl would become a target after Arseton saw him in the botanica. But that was a long time ago. I was convinced that Arseton's mission was to stake another vampire tonight.

I watched through Matt's eyes as the men dragged the zombie to the street and into the back of the van. No one in the ranch house or any of its neighbors came outside. Matt was the last to climb into the van, reluctant to get in there with a zombie.

But the zombie was poor, sweet Carl. He had never killed anyone and eaten their brains. As far as I knew. I'd rarely been afraid of him, and now he was going to be executed by a delusional fanatic.

From Courtney to Carl, it was not a good time to be a monster in Jellyfish Beach.

Two of the men sat on the zombie while Matt was ordered to hold his feet. The creature struggled, but he was tied securely by the rope.

"Where are we taking him?" asked the man who was holding the zombie's head down with the crowbar.

"The Angel Myron will reveal where we will sacrifice the monster."

"I hope he reveals it soon because this thing is strong. How do you kill a zombie, anyway? A shot to the head like they do it on TV?"

"Of course."

Matt should have stayed silent, but self-restraint has never been one of his virtues.

"So, why does this angel want us to kill monsters?" he asked. "Aren't there tons of humans on your hate list?"

"Yeah, when are we going to slay the people who just sit there at a green light?" asked the guy with the crowbar.

"We will slay whomever the angel commands us to slay," Arseton said in a dark voice. "For now, it is monsters, because they are abominations in the eyes of the Lord."

"Or is it because you get all the fun of killing without those pesky police detectives getting involved?" Matt asked.

The inside of the van fell silent.

"I believe Myron will give us permission to kill whom he deems to be the right human," Arseton said. "Or whom I deem to be the right one. New Guy, you don't look like any member I know. Who invited you into our order? Were you properly initiated?"

"You invited me, my lord. I know you must be too busy to remember everyone you talk to."

Arseton's eyes studied him in the rearview mirror.

"You know, now that I think about it, you *do* look familiar. Didn't I see you at last year's Renaissance festival? You were with a witch, I believe. A witch who has been a real annoyance lately."

"Wrong guy. I've got one of those faces that everyone thinks looks familiar."

"I will pray to the Angel Myron for permission to kill you tonight along with this monster."

Matt bolted for the rear door, but arms grabbed him and held him on the floor, next to the struggling zombie.

I couldn't drive while maintaining the magic connection with Matt. But I needed to follow the van. So, I sped off in pursuit of it, keeping my eyes on the road and losing my vision of what Matt was seeing.

The van didn't return to the hotel or go to Arseton's apartment. Instead, it headed west, leaving Jellyfish Beach. We passed gated subdivisions in what used to be farmland. The landscape became increasingly rural, though new developments popped up here and there in their inexorable push to swallow Crab County.

Soon, we would reach the northern fringes of the Everglades where development could go no further.

It was a perfect place to dump bodies.

The road heading west was straight as an arrow. I followed the van through the intersection of the last north-south thoroughfare. The road narrowed and traffic thinned. It was easy to keep an eye on the van now.

Until it wasn't. The van simply disappeared.

I picked up my speed but still couldn't see the van ahead. Only dirt roads branched off this one, and most had closed gates. I should have seen the van if it turned off, or at least the dust it kicked up going down the dirt roads.

I saw nothing. Where had the van gone? This was a flat, uninhabited landscape of vegetable fields and palmettos. There was no place to hide.

Cutting through the anxiety that filled me came a prickling sensation. It wasn't the familiar tingling in your scalp or chill down your spine. The prickling came from my solar plexus, in the core of my energies.

The witch in me was sensing magic in the air. Evil magic.

I didn't believe it came from Arseton; there'd been no sign he was a magician of any sort. The magic, I feared, came from the demon.

Was the demon aware of me?

A tomato-packing warehouse appeared on the left. I pulled off the main road and drove into the dirt parking lot that wrapped around the building. There was no van, no cars at all.

There were no doors large enough for the van to enter the building.

I couldn't believe the van had been able to lose me. Black magic must be why.

My only option was to reengage the spell connected to Matt. I parked in front of the packing house, with a view of the main road.

I cleared my mind, sensing for the tendrils of magic that connected me with the amulet and Matt. It was difficult to slow my racing heart and block out my anxieties. Soon, however, I was no longer in the dirt parking lot of the packing house, but in the rear of the van, where Matt was lying face-down on the metal floor with his hands and feet bound with zip ties. Carl continued to struggle beside him.

I couldn't tell where the van was because I was looking through Matt's eyes at the floor. But it was obvious the van was traveling down a bumpy, unpaved road.

"How will we slay them, my lord?" a man asked.

"We will take their heads, as the Angel Myron has commanded me."

"Take them where?" Matt quipped, the fact that his death was imminent not having sunken in yet.

Arseton laughed and the other men joined in.

Carl moaned.

Suddenly, my vision went black. It wasn't from Matt closing his eyes, but because all his senses were blocked from me.

A tiny speck of light appeared. It grew into a glowing orb that sped toward me, like a Roman candle shooting across the bleak nothingness of space.

As it grew larger, it revealed itself as an eyeball, its iris a pulsating yellow. It filled my vision and invaded my mind, blotting out my consciousness with its malevolence.

As it loomed over me like a planet about to smash me to bits, the reflection of a human face appeared in its black hole of a pupil. I screamed.

The human face I saw in the eyeball was mine.

CHAPTER 15

GET MY ZOMBIE BACK

Madame Tibodet glared at me as if it were my fault that her zombie had been stolen.

"You sent Carl on errands with no regard to the danger of him being discovered," I said. "This nut job, Arseton, came to the botanica and saw him."

"The nut job came here because of you," Madame Tibodet said in her lyrical Caribbean accent.

"It wasn't Missy's fault," Luisa said from behind the botanica's counter. "He has a vendetta against all things supernatural, and it was inevitable that he would come here."

"How are you going to get my zombie back?"

"How are *we* going to get him back?" Luisa asked angrily. "You're the one who controls him."

"They kidnapped a friend of mine, too," I said. "A living person has priority over a dead one."

"Carl is like family to me," said Madame Tibodet. "I've tried to summon him, but he hasn't returned."

"They tied him up with rope," I said. When I wondered why they used rope on Carl and zip ties on Matt, I had the sickening realization that the zip ties would have probably cut through the semi-decayed flesh.

"Do you have a way of locating him?" I asked.

I knew a couple of locating spells. For the best of them, I would need a beloved possession of Matt's, which I didn't have. The other spell was less accurate and relied on visually finding the white van. The problem was, it was apparent the demon had cloaked the van with invisibility.

"Voodoo isn't like your witchy magic," Madame Tibodet said. "I can't just wave a wand to find out where Carl is."

"For the record, I don't use a wand. Are you saying there's absolutely nothing you can do? This group of crazies is going to kill my friend and make Carl dead again. Permanently dead."

"I can pray to the loas. If they choose to help me, they might tell me where Carl and your friend are."

"Don't you have any magic that can search for them?" I asked. "Wouldn't you have a link to Carl since you created him?"

"No, I did not create him," she said adamantly. "I am not a *caplata*."

When she saw my confused look, she added. "I am not a sorceress. I am a *manbo*, a priestess, who worships the loas and the spirits of our departed loved ones, helping my clients communicate with them."

"I thought you were a sorceress. I thought you created Carl to work for you."

Anger flashed in Madame Tibodet's eyes. Unlike at the moment, I was usually pretty good at not offending people, especially those with different backgrounds from mine. It's a quality I learned from nursing.

"Carl was not created to be my slave. Carl is my brother."

Both Luisa and I gasped in surprise. "I'm so sorry," I said.

"He was murdered after we came to America. While his soul was waiting for permission from the loas to pass to the afterlife, a *bokor*—a male sorcerer—turned him into a zombie. The bokor offered to sell him to me. If I said no, Carl would have been sold to someone else to be their slave. I couldn't allow that to happen to my brother, so I bought him from the bokor. I considered hiring the bokor to release Carl from his undead existence, to let him die again and go to heaven." Tears streamed down her cheeks. "But I couldn't lose my brother a second time."

"Carl is a very sweet zombie," Luisa said.

"I have him run errands for me, not as my slave, but because he needs to be kept busy. It makes him happier. And if you're wondering why he lives in a shed, instead of in my house, come on. He's a zombie! I have grandchildren there. And some of my clients come to my house. Carl doesn't have the best, you know, body odor. He was perfectly comfortable in the shed."

"This only makes it more important that we find your brother and my friend. And we need to do it quickly," I said.

"I know. I'm praying to the loas and hope one will possess me and show me the way."

"I think you should ask the bokor who reanimated Carl," Luisa said.

"I don't believe he could track down a zombie he made so long ago. He's made too many to keep track. Half the members of the Florida Legislature are zombies he created. I would rather not have anything more to do with that evil sorcerer."

I could understand how she felt because of my birth mother. You don't want to associate with someone practicing black magic and get their foul stench on you.

That's why I accepted the fact I would need to use my own witchery—benign, white magic—to find Matt and Carl. And it wouldn't be easy.

We hugged Madame Tibodet and gave her our promises that we would find Carl. The bells above the door rang when she left. They sounded mournful this time.

◖◗◖◗◖◗◖◗

I ASKED Luisa if she had ever heard of a demon that manifests itself as a disembodied floating eyeball.

"No, but I'm sure it has nothing to do with the Illuminati."

"What are you talking about?"

"The Eye of Providence, like on the back of the dollar bill. It's a popular symbol of the Freemasons and the Illuminati, who are everywhere in internet conspiracy theories nowadays. But they don't have a demon."

"How would you know?"

"My neighbor's a member of the Illuminati. They don't need a demon because they already control the entire world."

"Of course, they do," I said. "Anyway, I did a little research on the demon, and it doesn't resemble any of the popular ones in the demonology literature. The best I could determine is that it's a cacodemon, a run-of-the-mill demon. What's curious is that Arseton says the demon is telling him to destroy supernatural creatures. Why would it want him to do that? You'd think a demon would be simpatico with monsters."

"Ah, maybe that's the issue: the monsters are not simpatico with this demon and others. I can't speak for everywhere, but here in Jellyfish Beach, monsters have been Americanized. They exist hidden from most humans, but they live human-style lives."

"Yeah," I said. "Vampires shopping with coupons at Mega-Mart—how more American can you get?"

"Exactly. Monsters here just want to live comfortable lives. They're not interested in being evil like the monsters of my grandparents' era. It could be that this demon isn't happy about that. It wants monsters to be evil again."

"That makes sense. Mrs. Lupis and Mr. Lopez suggested the demon might want to flush monsters out of hiding and create chaos. Maybe it just wants them to pledge fealty to the demon and start being evil again, while it dupes Arseton into thinking he's a warrior fighting them."

"Yeah," Luisa said. "It kind of makes sense in a crazy way."

"Except I don't know how the demon is getting this message across to the monsters. Is it communicating with them?"

"Could be. Or simply having humans kill them will make them want to kill humans to protect themselves. It creates a cycle of violence and makes the monsters evil, at least in the eyes of humans."

"That means more monsters will reveal their existence to humans."

"And the monsters will be slaughtered. How would that benefit the demon?"

The bells atop the front door tinkled, and Mrs. Lupis and Mr. Lopez walked into the botanica wearing their usual gray business suits.

"The demon will become stronger from all the death and destruction," Mr. Lopez said.

"As well as the fear and hatred," said Mrs. Lupis. "True, many monsters will be lost, but many more will be created in this war of good versus evil."

"How the heck do you guys know what we're talking about and always show up at the appropriate moment?" Luisa asked.

"Intuition," Mr. Lopez said.

"You guys are supernaturals, aren't you?" I asked.

"We're normal human beings," said Mrs. Lupis.

"You've got some supernatural or paranormal in you," Luisa said. "My intuition tells me so."

My witchy intuition told me the same thing. There was definitely some magic in the air whenever the two members of the Friends of Cryptids Society of the Americas walked in.

"Did you guys come by just to finish our conversation for us?"

"We came to encourage you to stop the Knights Simplar," Mrs. Lupis replied, showing no effects from Luisa's sarcasm.

"Is a zombie really that important to you?" Luisa asked.

"Don't forget," I said, "they have my friend, Matt, too."

"Yeah, sorry."

"The Knights Simplar is a deranged cult," Mr. Lopez said. "They have no right to exterminate strange beings or supernatural creatures."

That was the perfect way to describe Matt and Carl.

"Did the Knights Simplar stake two vampires recently?" I asked.

The two liaisons looked at me strangely.

"You know about the stakings?" Mrs. Lupis asked.

"Of course I do. I'm really tight with the vampires in this community. How do you know about them?"

"We know everything involving monsters," Mr. Lopez said.

His partner added, "We thought the stakings were vampire disciplinary actions."

"No. They were murders."

"Then there's even more reason to protect the vampires by stopping Lord Arseton," Mr. Lopez said. "The undocumented species that is in Squid Tower must be protected, too. Obviously, you've made no progress in identifying it."

At last, one of them exhibited emotion. Mr. Lopez was clearly disappointed with me.

"I still don't see why you guys can't find the creature if you know everything else that's going on around here," Luisa said.

"Because we have partners like you," Mrs. Lupis said with a snarky grin. Today was a breakthrough day in emoting for these guys.

"Before you use magic to locate your friend, be wary of reporting his kidnapping to the police," Mr. Lopez said to me.

"How did you know I was going to use magic?"

"It fits your profile."

"Why should I be wary of the police? If I can get Lord Arseton charged with false imprisonment, it will put him behind bars before he can kill my friend and the zombie. Not that I have the time to fill out police paperwork."

"Exactly," Mrs. Lupis said. "You need to find them quickly before they're killed. The police won't be fast enough. And contacting the police will violate our most important unwritten rule."

"What rule is that?"

"Don't contact the police," Mr. Lopez said. "Not when there's the possibility of them encountering a monster. The police cannot know about monsters because it won't end well. Not for the police, and not for the monsters."

"I believe my magic can help me find my friend, but don't think I can stop the cult on my own."

"We don't simply show up to make cryptic statements," Mrs. Lupis said with the nearest thing to a smile she'd ever exhibited. "We have assets who can assist you. When you locate your friend, text this number."

She handed me a business card. On the front was simply her name. On the rear was a handwritten phone number.

"You need to get to work immediately. You have very little time. Which is why we are leaving now."

She and Mr. Lopez gave us a curt nod and slipped out the door.

"Those two give me the creeps," Luisa said.

"Yeah, there's a lot of stuff that needs to be explained. But I've got work to do now."

"Yes, girl, do your *bruja* thing."

I DROVE to Matt's bungalow to get a possession of his to use in my locator spell. I couldn't go inside without wasting time with a spell to unlock the door, but in an adjoining shed were his fishing rods and a new paddleboard. The latter was infused with the passionate but often short-lived love we have for our newest toys. Perfect for my spell.

I performed the spell right there in Matt's tiny backyard, drawing my magic circle in the dirt with a stick. After gathering my energies and those of the elements, I directed my magic at the paddleboard, animating Matt's energy he had left on it.

Soon, a glowing orb created by his energy hovered at eye level. I bonded it to my own energy, allowing me to have visual contact with the orb. It was like the spell that allowed me to share Matt's senses, but with this spell, I didn't need to be near the orb like I'd had to with Matt's amulet.

When I was connected to the orb, I commanded it to find and rejoin the source of Matt's energy—Matt himself.

The orb sailed away to the west. It traveled too quickly for me to see where it was going, but I assumed it would travel to a place near where I lost contact with the van. The orb should be able to find it, even if the demon's magic made it invisible.

Minutes passed, more than should have elapsed since I'd sent the orb on its way. I tried to sense if it was still traveling, but all I received was darkness and static. But I waited. There was nothing else I could do.

Finally, a blurry vision came to me. The orb was hovering above a river in a dense forest. As the vision came into focus, I spotted alligators basking on the sand and mud banks of the river. White egrets perched in the branches of an oak tree.

But the van wasn't there, nor were any signs of Carl or Matt.

Until my eyes made sense of the jumble of trees, grass, and cypress knees at the water's edge. One of the cypress knees protruding from the bank, inches from the water's edge—and only a few yards from a gator—looked odd.

I gasped when I realized what it was.

Matt's head and shoulders, poking up from the mud.

He'd been buried alive.

CHAPTER 16

UP TO HIS NECK IN ALLIGATORS

T
didn't need to compare the visual provided by the orb with a satellite map to narrow down the location. I recognized the unique scenery from past kayaking expeditions, many of which had been with Matt.

Matt was buried in a bank of the Loxahatchee River, specifically the upstream freshwater portion.

I didn't know if Arseton's plan was to wait for gators to eat Matt's head, or whether Arseton was going to execute him himself. All I knew was I needed to rescue him immediately and save Carl, too, if he was still "alive."

But how?

Mr. Lopez and Mrs. Lupis said I couldn't call the police if there was a chance they would encounter Carl. Well, the Friends of Cryptids could go take a long walk off a short pier. They could claw back their funding if they wanted, but I would not ignore the police when Matt's life was in danger.

But wait. A scenario ran through my head of police helicopters buzzing over the forest, forcing Arseton to shoot Matt and make his escape. Then, a SWAT team finding Carl and blowing him away out of fear.

Or, even worse, the police not believing me when I told them fanatics were going to kill my friend because a demon told them to.

The business card Mrs. Lupis gave me was still in my pocket.

"We will back you up," she had said.

I texted a message to the number on the back of the card that I had found Matt and needed help.

The reply came almost instantly.

Angela Davie is our local field agent. She will meet you at the canoe launch in the state park. Go now, and don't call the police.

Really? One person would be enough to help me take on the Knights Simplar? It looked like I was going to find out.

I quickly threw my kayak atop my car and strapped it to the rack. When I say "quickly," it included the time spent swearing like a sailor as I lifted the boat to the roof—which gets harder every year—and swearing again when I accidentally banged the kayak into the door panel. Good thing my car was long past the condition where a little ding would make a difference.

It took nearly an hour to drive to the park. Every minute was filled with anxiety about Matt and Carl. I tried to keep my mind focused on preparing the magic I might use if Angela and I encountered the Knights Simplar.

I'm not like a wizard or mage with an arsenal of magical pyrotechnics. I'm a humble earth witch who cares more about healing than fighting. Though, at times like this, I wish I had more spells that could be weaponized.

I had a decent protection spell to keep me physically safe and a warding spell to fend off some magical attacks. My sleep spell could take down most humans, and you already saw the effectiveness of my laxative spell.

What I couldn't do was make an opponent's heart or head explode, though I admit I'd fantasized about it when someone cut me off in traffic. Could I shoot fireballs and lightning bolts? Nope and nope.

I hoped Angela carried some serious firepower. After all, there were only two of us. Perhaps, it was wishful thinking, but I imagined Angela to be like a heroine in the urban fantasy novels I read: young, fit and adept in martial arts, sword fighting, and heavy weaponry. Possibly magic, too. Or, even better, she was a shifter who turned into a grizzly bear.

When I arrived at the park, the canoe and kayak rental stand had already closed, so I was glad I brought my kayak. There was only one other car in the parking lot—a giant American sedan from another era. Arseton's rental van was nowhere to be found.

As I was undoing the straps that held my kayak to the roof rack, a voice came from behind me.

"Hello, I'm Angela."

"Hi," I said as I turned around. "I'm Miss—"

"Miss Marple?"

The smiling woman was old and slight, white hair in a bun, a librarian. And I don't mean like a librarian. I recognized her as *the* librarian of the Jellyfish Beach Public Library, though she was well past retirement age. At least she was wearing appropriate clothing: hat, shorts, water shoes, and a vented fishing shirt.

I found it extremely difficult to imagine this woman doing a backflip while wielding a sword.

"Missy," I said. "I'm Missy."

"Nice to meet you. Let's go search for your friend, shall we? My canoe is already in the water."

She helped me take my kayak down from the roof, which couldn't have been easy for someone as dainty as she, so I felt a little better. Maybe she'd turn out to be a grizzly shifter or something after all.

"So," I said as we prepared to launch, "you're a member of the Friends of Cryptids Society?"

"Yep. And a part-time employee."

"What, exactly, do you do? You keep records of the various monsters?"

"Yes, I do. And I'm also the enforcer for this district of Florida."

"Enforcer?"

"Yes. When monsters go rogue, threaten to reveal themselves, or eat people, I make them think twice about doing it again. In rare cases, I put them down."

"Wow." I stole a glance at the grandmother librarian. "You?"

"Yes. It's kind of refreshing after working a desk job all day."

By now, we were floating downstream along the river that wound through dense stands of oak, gumbo limbo, palmetto, and towering cypress trees. Wading birds, such as egrets and herons, perched on fallen logs. And the occasional alligator snoozed on the banks, half in and half out of the water.

Angela handled her canoe expertly as the current swept us

along. From previous trips, I knew there were a couple of small waterfalls downstream before the river widened as it neared the ocean, and the trees turned into mangroves as saltwater from the tides mixed with the fresh.

I believed we didn't have to travel that far. Matt was buried somewhere in this upper portion of the river, based on the image from the orb. We had to find him soon. The sunlight glinting sideways through the trees meant daylight would end soon.

And darkness meant the alligators would begin to feed.

ᚲ୯ᑀᑀ୯୰

THE RIVERBANKS WERE COVERED with vegetation, fallen logs, and cypress knees—the vertical knobs that protruded from the ground as part of the cypress trees' root systems. It would be more difficult than I had realized to spot Matt along the miles of river we'd have to cover before the topography changed.

Matt's amulet must have fallen off, or the demon was still blocking my original surveillance spell. Instead, I needed to reactivate the locator spell into a simplified version that would allow me to zero in on Matt's energy concentration.

"Angela, could you tow my kayak for a little while? I guess it's okay to tell you, since you're a member of the Society, but I'm a witch. I need to focus on a spell right now to locate Matt."

"Yes, they told me about you," she said. "I'll tie a line to the carry handle on your bow. You'll be easy to tow going downstream."

After she connected my kayak to hers, I placed my paddle in

my lap and cleared my mind, gathered my energies, and felt for remnants of the magic I'd used to search for Matt. The orb was gone, its energy absorbed into Matt. Fortunately, the framework of the spell I had created hadn't completely faded yet. Like the wooden framing of a home, it was still there, attached to the field of magic that surrounded me during periods when I'm actively casting spells.

Supported by this framework, I sent out tendrils of energy searching.

Memories, scents, images of Matt came to me. It meant he was nearby. I wouldn't be able to locate him as precisely as the orb had, but this would help.

However, as we continued down the river, the images of Matt faded.

"I think we passed him," I said. "Somehow, we went by without seeing him. We have to backtrack."

It took powerful paddle thrusts to turn around. Going against the current, Angela could no longer tow me easily, so I had to paddle my kayak. My sense of Matt grew stronger now, but the keenness of my perceptions faded as my exertions caused me to lose contact with my spell.

"He must be unconscious if he didn't call out when we paddled by him," Angela said.

I nodded. I didn't mention the other possibility—that he was dead.

We agreed Angela would search the left bank and I would study the right. As the day faded, I used a flashlight and studied every object on the bank: cypress knees, coconuts, turtles atop logs, alligators.

There, up ahead, the muddy sand looked disturbed. It could

be from an alligator wallowing, or it could be from a shovel digging. I paddled closer to shore.

Behind a cypress knee was an object that looked like a coconut. As I drifted closer, I bathed it in my flashlight's beam.

It was the head of a man buried up to his shoulders in the bank.

"Matt! We'll get you out."

Swimming parallel to my kayak was an alligator heading directly toward Matt, propelled by its powerful tail. There was no time to throw a protection spell around my friend.

"Get out of here!" I screamed, slapping the water with my paddle.

The alligator dove and disappeared into the dark water, hopefully for good.

Angela and I paddled our crafts into the shallow water and onto a beach of sorts where the bank flattened at the water's edge.

Matt was unconscious. I pressed my fingers against his carotid artery to make sure he had a pulse, then frantically clawed the sand away from him with my hands.

"Use the head of your paddle, dear."

I grabbed my paddle and used it like a shovel. Though the paddle head was plastic, the wet, muddy sand was soft enough not to break it. Angela dug beside me with her canoe paddle.

We soon had enough sand excavated from around Matt to see that he was in a sitting position, still wearing his tunic, his legs folded close to his chest. As we dug at the sand above his legs, something came crunching through the woods toward us.

A man wearing a white tunic stepped out of the trees, aiming a handgun at us.

"Get out of here," he said. "This is private property."

"This is a state park, and you're trying to murder this man."

"I don't want to shoot you."

He didn't get to. His gun flew from his hand and landed in the river.

"What the?" He stared at his hand in amazement.

It wasn't my magic that did it. I glanced at Angela.

"Where's the zombie?" she asked the man.

He pulled a hunting knife from beneath his tunic. And his tunic promptly caught on fire. He screamed and tried to bat it out.

Then, he rose in the air, glided over the river where he hung suspended.

"Tell me where the zombie is, and I'll douse the flames," Angela commanded.

The man whimpered. "I don't know. They took it away in the van after we buried this guy."

"Where do you think they were taking the zombie?"

"I don't know! I'm burning!"

He dropped into the river and went under. His wet, balding head quickly popped above the surface like a turtle's.

"I'm sure they discussed where they were taking the zombie," Angela said.

"They left me here to guard this guy. They didn't tell me where they were going afterward."

Angela stretched her arms out toward the river and raised them, palms up.

"Dinner time!" she called.

Pairs of prehistoric eyes and nostrils appeared and formed a semicircle around the Knight Simplar.

"No!" the man cried, swimming toward the shore.

Angela pointed an outstretched hand at him, and what looked like a blue lightning bolt shot from her fingers, knocking him backward.

This was exactly the kind of magic I wished I could do. How can my sleep spell compare to cooler-than-anything stuff like this?

"If you want to get out of the water before the gators get you, all you have to do is talk."

The alligators inched closer to him. He squealed, and his head went down, then up again. He spat out water as he became too tired to stay afloat.

"You'd better save some oxygen for when a gator takes you under in a death-roll."

"Okay, okay! They're taking him to some voodoo store on Sixth Street. They're going to kill him and burn his body at the stake there to attract a lot of attention and force the store to be closed."

"It's not just a voodoo store," I said. "We also carry supplies for Santeria, obeah, hoodoo, Wicca, general witchcraft—"

"Get me out of here!" he shrieked.

Angela made a lifting motion with her hands, and the man rose a few feet above the water just as a gator lunged at him. She held him suspended there while another gator snapped at his feet before finally moving him over dry land.

"We need to keep him here and report the attempted murder to the police," I said. "I know a good binding spell."

"Rope will do just fine. You don't want the police having to undo your magic."

"If you can handle that, I'll tend to Matt."

Angela lowered the man to the ground and kept him immobile with her magic while she hogtied him with rope from her canoe. I finished uncovering Matt from the sand and performed the most thorough exam of him I could do with no medical instruments.

I found nothing wrong with him, no injury that would have left him unconscious. Either he'd been drugged, or Arseton knew some magic. I truly dreaded the latter possibility.

I was glad Angela had a canoe because my kayak only sat one person, and it would be difficult to strap Matt atop it. After we loaded him into the canoe, I texted Luisa and warned her about the Knights Simplar's plan to burn Carl at the botanica.

I'll ask Mme. Tibodet to help me keep watch over the place. But it would be best if we found him still undead, she responded.

I assured her I would do all I could.

Angela and I paddled back to the boat launch. We agreed we would wait until we left the park before calling the police to come pick up the bad guy. I didn't have time to spend half the night being interviewed by them.

Now that we were paddling upstream, the going was much tougher. Angela somehow kept up with me, despite the extra weight in the bow of her canoe.

"You're a much more powerful witch than I," I said.

"I've reached mage status in this late stage of life," she said. "But power isn't everything in magic. Intelligence and compassion are important, too."

"Your magic is why the Society assigned you as an enforcer?"

"Exactly."

"What do you make of Mr. Lopez and Mrs. Lupis? They're

really strange. It's creepy the way they suddenly show up when you're talking about them."

I hoped Angela wasn't offended by my comment.

"Yes. I believe they might not be fully human," she said.

"What do you mean?"

"I don't know. There is much about the Society you will learn in time, but some things we'll never know."

It was too dark now to read her face.

"Row, row, row your boat gently up the stream," sang a male voice in Angela's canoe. He sounded drunk.

"Matt! Are you okay?" I asked.

"I'm a little groggy. Why are my clothes all wet?"

"Long story. Did they drug you?"

"I don't remember. Well, when they had me on the floor of the van, I felt a sharp pain in my butt cheek."

"What was the last thing you remember?"

"The sharp pain in my butt cheek,"

"Hypodermic needle," I said. "Did you hear them discuss any plans?"

"Just to kill me and Carl. I guess I should say, re-kill Carl. Or make him dead again. Or deader. Anyway, if they talked about anything else, I didn't hear it. I wasn't really listening after the part about them killing us."

"We have to find them. They still have Carl and plan to burn his body at the botanica to get us in trouble."

"Why didn't they kill me?"

"Because we came along," Angela said.

"Oh, thank you. Didn't see you behind me. I was wondering why this canoe was moving when I wasn't paddling it. My name is Matt."

"I'm Angela."

"Wait, aren't you the librarian in Jellyfish Beach?"

"I am. And if you're awake enough to talk so much, perhaps you can help me with the paddling?"

"Uh, yeah. Sure."

Angela reached forward to hand him an extra paddle. He fumbled it, dropping it in the water.

"Sorry, I'm still kinda out of it."

"I understand," she said, scooping up the paddle. "Try again."

This time, Matt was able to paddle, although awkwardly.

"Luisa told me there's no sign of the van at the botanica," I said, returning my phone to my pocket. "We need to find them before they kill Carl, if they haven't done so already. I have no direct connection with them. My magic can't find them."

"Mine can't, either" Angela said.

"I'm hungry," Matt said.

I fought back the urge to say something bitingly sarcastic about his dumb comment. My urge prevailed.

"Of course. It's dinnertime. What else would a man be thinking about?"

"Fast food," Matt said.

"Really? At a time like this?"

"I remember now that there were fast-food wrappers all over the floor of the van. My face was on top of one. Fried chicken sandwich. You know that chain. Arseton must really like it. Maybe we should drive by that restaurant or other fast-food places. If you're taking a break from manual labor with other dudes, you're not going to going to stop at a salad joint."

"There are dozens of fast-foot restaurants between here

and Jellyfish Beach," I said. "We couldn't possibly drive to all of them. Besides, they could have eaten already. Or maybe they won't eat at all."

"An army marches on its stomach. Arseton would be in a hurry to complete his plans at the botanica, so I would start by checking out the restaurants near it. Then, fan out from there."

I didn't have a better plan. So, once we loaded up our boats on our cars, we drove back to Jellyfish Beach. I hoped we'd get lucky.

MATT SPRAWLED in the passenger seat, his hair wet, his face streaked with sandy mud. His sunken eyes peering from beneath his dirty brows reminded me of photos of soldiers at war. He had nearly lost his life, and it was probably just sinking in for him.

My heart did a little backflip. This cute, irascible guy almost died helping me in yet another of my crazy supernatural misadventures. He hadn't done this for his career, or for any financial gain. It was all just to help me.

And what was his reward? Mud, blood, and a near alligator attack. Plus, instead of resting, he had to spend the evening tracking down bad guys and possibly fighting them.

My heart, hidden behind the scar tissue of loss and disappointment, opened for once. Maybe I could fall in love with Matt after all.

Not quite yet, though. I still feared opening myself to

possible pain. Being vulnerable, becoming dependent on someone else, still frightened me too much.

But who knows? Perhaps there *was* room for Matt in my future.

"Hey," I said. He looked up at me. "Thanks for putting your life at risk for us. For me."

He smiled, his teeth white amid the shadows and mud.

"It's what I do. Crazy stuff with Missy."

CHAPTER 17

SHOPPING CENTER SHOWDOWN

You must believe me that Jellyfish Beach is a picturesque town. Founded along the tracks of the Florida East Coast Railroad in the late 1800s, the downtown spreads east from the tracks to the Intracoastal Waterway and continues over the bridge to the beach. It's quaint and lovely.

But, just like any municipality in the US, it's surrounded by strip malls, shopping centers, and, yes, fast-food joints. More than I ever realized until we drove by each and every one of them in Angela's giant grandmother-style car after I dropped mine off at home.

We started with the fried chicken sandwich place that Arseton obviously loved. The white van wasn't there. Then, on to various burger places amid clouds of greasy smoke. Next came fake Mexican, pizza, Asian, Latin, Greek, fried seafood, over-priced coffee, donuts, even a place specializing in hotdogs.

No white van.

"I guess they ate already," Matt said.

"Or Lord Arseton invited them to his apartment for a home-cooked meal of crazy casserole," I said. "If we can't find them soon, we'll need to guard the botanica. I'd rather not confront them there, because if the police show up, we'll have the outcome Arseton wants: a dead zombie at a botanica."

We cruised past a sushi restaurant in a large strip mall. At one end of the plaza was a laundromat.

I looked down at my sand-and-mud-stained shirt and shorts and remembered how filthy the white tunic was of the guy we captured. That's what happens when you bury a man alive in a riverbank. Matt's tunic was completely soiled, too, of course.

"Let's check out the parking area near that laundromat," I said. Lord Arseton seemed like the type who preferred to perform his ritual slayings neatly attired.

We all gasped when we saw the white van. We drove past it at a safe distance. One man was in the front seat, wearing a T-shirt without his tunic. He must have been there to guard Carl, who, hopefully, was inside. He stared at his phone, oblivious to us.

Arseton had three "volunteers" plus Matt when they first set off to capture Carl. Subtracting Matt and the guy we tied up at the river meant Arseton had only two men. One was in the van. Therefore, Arseton was in the laundromat with only one soldier.

"I'm sure that guy locked himself in, so no sense in storming the van," I said. "I don't know if he has the keys or if

Arseton does. So, I think the best approach is for Angela and me to go into the laundromat and neutralize Arseton and the other guy. If one of them has the keys, we'll bring them out. But just in case they don't, Matt, you stay out here and make sure that guy doesn't take off in the van."

Angela handed him her car keys. "If that guy tries to leave, chase him," she said.

I told them it would be better if I used my sleep spell on the man. Concentrating while I gathered my energies, I recited the incantation and sent the magic toward its target, penetrating the glass. The man slumped forward against the dashboard.

"If the guy wakes up and tries to come into the laundromat," I continued, "stop him."

"Gladly," Matt said. "That guy stomped on my neck when I was in the van."

"How do we 'neutralize' them in the laundromat in front of the other people?" Angela asked. "I see at least two others in there."

"I'll use my sleeping spell on the civilians. Then, you can go to town with your magic on the bad guys."

Matt remained in Angela's car while she and I approached the brightly lit laundromat. To avoid being seen, we split up and approached it from the sides.

I arrived first. Peering through the windows, I saw Arseton supervising his subordinate as he dumped wet tunics in a dryer. Arseton thrust a box of fabric softener at him. In the front of the room, an elderly man sat in a plastic chair, reading a magazine. A young male attendant swept up in the back.

I conjured my sleeping spell. In less than a minute, the old man was asleep with his chin on his chest. The attendant passed out in a closet, his splayed-out feet extending from the doorway.

Angela stood outside the laundromat, opposite me. I gave her a nod.

She stepped in front of the glass, pointed with both hands, and the two Knights Simplar abruptly froze.

"How do you do that?" I asked. "My spells require all sorts of rituals."

"Most witches are like you. If you want to get to my level, it will take a lot of training. But your magic is just fine."

We went inside, past the snoring old man. My sleep spell works pretty well. So what if I have to recite the spell and can't just point?

Arseton and his goon stood unmoving in front of the open, industrial-sized dryer, a dryer sheet dangling from Arseton's hand. They looked like domestic partners in an ad for fabric softener.

I patted down their pockets. It was impossible to miss the handgun that each had tucked in their back waistbands. I removed them carefully and placed them in a trashcan. The key fob for the van was in Arseton's front right pocket. I shuddered with revulsion when I reached in to retrieve it.

"How long does your sleep spell last?" Angela asked.

"This one should last for an hour, at least."

"My immobility spell will wear off in half that time, but we should be long gone by then. Let's see if the zombie is okay, then return him to his home."

Before we left, I couldn't resist a symbolic gesture. I pushed

Arseton into the open dryer with the tunics and shut the glass door. Only the nurse in me stopped me from turning on the machine.

That was easy. Almost too easy, I thought as we strolled out into the parking lot. When we approached the van, I waved to Matt in Angela's car and gave him a thumbs-up. He jumped out and joined us as I clicked the key fob and unlocked the van.

I yanked open the rear doors. Carl was still on the floor, tied securely.

"Carl, are you okay?"

He moaned in response. It was a cheerful moan. My sleep spell had been targeted at the driver only.

"Let's take Carl in the van," Matt said. "No sense leaving it here to make it easy for those guys to come after us. Even if we throw away this key fob, they might have the spare somewhere."

"Good idea. Okay, Carl, we're taking you home to your sister now."

Famous last words.

Because Myron the angel—who was really a demon —showed up.

αρροσαρο

THE EYEBALL, now as large as a yoga ball, hovered above us, illuminated with light from within. It looked rather bloodshot compared to the last time I'd seen it. Maybe, it wasn't getting enough sleep or needed reading glasses.

"Not him again," Angela said.

"You know him?" I asked.

"He regularly harasses our monsters and tries to turn them evil."

Myron was done with our small talk. He rotated to face Matt, but the eyeball embroidered on Matt's tunic, however dirty, assured the demon that Matt was on his team. Now, he turned toward me. A burning sensation spread from my toes, through my feet, up my legs to my torso. My knees buckled, and I dropped painfully to a kneeling position.

Submit to me. The words echoed in my head in a cartoon voice, like someone who just inhaled helium.

Ouch! Was the next thing I heard, right after Angela blasted him with blue lightning. The burning inside me lessened.

"Help me, Missy," Angela said. "We need both our powers to have a fighting chance against a demon."

"But I can't—"

"You have power. You *must* use it in this fight."

Angela gasped and sank to her knees like I had.

As I told you before, I don't use my magic for fighting. Before I could figure out how to get on the offensive, I used my power in a way that was very dependable: a protection spell. I cast it around both Angela and me, forming an invisible bubble that would keep out physical objects and some forms of magic.

I knew how to cast the spell quickly, or else it wouldn't be very protective, would it? Once the bubble had formed, much of the burning inside me went away.

I was pleased that my magic had some utility against the demon. But it wasn't enough to fend him off. I had to go on the attack.

Long ago, I learned I could perform a bit of telekinesis—the ability to move objects with your mind. It wasn't powerful enough to do anything other than party tricks, but the ability was enhanced by my magic. I couldn't pick up people and move them around like Angela could. Smaller things, however, were not a problem.

I ran away from the van with the demon floating after me.

Scattered across the parking lot were the opened shells of the nut-like pods that grow on mahogany trees. Developers in Florida loved to plant mahogany trees in parking lots for shade, even though the falling shells could ding car roofs.

I launched a hailstorm of shells at the demon. They blew in a concentrated gust and struck the demon without ceasing.

Incarnated as an eyeball, he didn't have the thickest skin.

The shriek of a banshee echoed across the parking lot as Myron was shot full of shells. The eyeball zipped into the air and disappeared. Which was a good thing, because three teenagers on skateboards had drifted over, attracted by the commotion.

"Good job," Angela said. "Get ready. He'll be back. Will the protection spell move with us?"

"Yes."

"Let's go back into the laundromat for shelter."

"Hey, what about me?" Matt asked.

"The demon won't hurt you because he thinks you're on his team. Stay out here and look after Carl."

Angela and I sprinted toward the laundromat. The four people inside, visible through the windows, were still unmoving, but for how much longer, I didn't know.

We made it inside just in the nick of time.

A tidal wave of flames hit the front of the laundromat, disappearing before the building caught fire.

"Myron sure is mad," I said.

It was safer in here, but the problem was we couldn't see where Myron was and thus couldn't shoot magic at him.

The lights went out.

"Great," I said. "Just like in a horror movie."

"Can you put your protection bubble around the building?" Angela asked.

"I can put it around a small structure like my house, but not this giant strip mall. I can protect the roof, the front and back, and this wall here since we're at the end of the building. This interior wall opposite won't have the same protection."

The electricity came back on in a big surge. The ceiling fans spun like airplane propellors, and all the washing machines and dryers turned on. A loud *thunk-thunk-thunk* came from the dryer in which Arseton was getting tumbled.

"We need to combine our power," Angela said. "Individually, we can't defeat the demon, but together, we have a shot."

"How?"

"Hold my hand. Gather all your energies and concentrate them. Then, I'll tap into them and use the extra power in my spells."

You remember that interior wall I mentioned? It buckled inward, and the drywall began breaking apart.

A giant, two-headed reptile butted its head through the wall. Myron's eyeball form, which was handy for impressing gullible cult members, was not useful in this situation. Transforming into the double reptile heads worked a lot better for him.

Fire shot from the two mouths, torching a table with someone's carefully folded laundry.

The wall fell away as the reptile pushed further into the room. Its body looked like that of a Nile monitor lizard and was as big as a city bus.

Still holding hands, Angela and I leaped to the side to escape another torrent of flames.

These were not exactly the best circumstances for concentrating, which I needed to do to gather my energies.

Angela released my hand and dashed past the breach in the wall, firing her blue lightning at the demon. I'd never seen a non-vampire of her age move so quickly. It was too risky, but it drew the demon's attention away from me so I could focus on my energies.

I can't say my stress was reduced, but I felt the surge of power grow inside me. I concentrated it into a dense ball of power in my solar plexus.

Another burst of flames hit the change machine, spilling quarters all over the floor.

Someone came up behind me. It was Angela.

"Ready?" she whispered.

I nodded, and she took my hand.

Pushing the power from my center and through my arm, I felt it flow into Angela's hand, leaving me depleted. But she positively glowed with the added power.

The giant reptile turned its two heads toward us, opened its mouths, and—

Two giant bolts of purple lightning shot from Angela's hands straight into the beast's mouths.

The air crackled with electricity. The smell of ozone filled the air, stronger even than the smoldering ashes.

The demon cocked its heads with confused expressions.

Then, the heads exploded.

There was no mess, though. The giant reptile had simply vanished.

"Did you kill him?"

"No," Angela said in a tired voice. "I sent Myron back to Hell, but he will return. Hopefully, not tonight."

We made our way through the ruins out of the laundromat, passing the teenagers gathered at the door.

"Whoa, dude, did you see that giant lizard?"

"No, you're just hallucinating."

The dryer continued to tumble-dry Arseton. His goon remained standing, frozen, beside it. Then, the fire sprinklers went off.

My only regret was I didn't get the chance to interrogate Arseton about whether he staked the vampires. Not that he would have answered me honestly. But at the moment, he was obsessed with zombies.

The next time he appeared uninvited in my life, I would ask him questions and maybe use my truth spell on him. In the meantime, I will make sure I haven't missed any other angles.

Blaring sirens approached. I smiled to myself, imagining what Arseton would say to the police when they surveyed the damage to the laundromat and asked him about the purpose of his strange tunic.

Our work here was done. Matt drove the van, and I rode shotgun. Angela followed us to Madame Tibodet's home. On the way, I texted Luisa, asking her to tell the priestess that we were bringing her brother home and to meet us there.

When we arrived, Madame Tibodet greeted us. It wasn't exactly an emotional reunion with hugging and sobbing, Carl being a zombie and all, but his sister shed some tears and hugged us.

But I couldn't savor the homecoming. I had a lot of work to do before Courtney stood trial.

CHAPTER 18
MR. BOKOR

When I passed the card room, Beatrice flagged me down. I went inside, where she was playing cards with Henrietta, Gladys, and Gloria.

"You're just the person we need to talk to, with your medical background," Beatrice said. "We were mentioning how we've all been so run-down lately. My husband says he feels more dead than undead."

"Not to state the obvious, but being turned at an older age will deny you the pep the vampires with younger body ages have," I said, a little too quickly.

"It's not that," Henrietta said. Agnes's right-hand woman spoke with an authority that couldn't be ignored. "This fatigue has come recently. I've never gotten so tired so easily before."

"Are you all taking your supplemental vitamins?"

Yes, even vampires need supplements when their body ages are over sixty.

"Yes, yes," Gladys said, waving a hand dismissively. "They don't do diddly."

"Have you been drinking whole blood, not just bags of plasma?"

They all grunted in the affirmative, losing patience at my lack of an instant diagnosis.

"Do any of you have a fever?" I approached Beatrice to put my hand on her forehead. "Do you mind?"

"Go ahead. I'm sure I don't have a fever. Haven't had one since I was a human."

It was rare for vampires to get fevers, since they weren't susceptible to most of the viruses or infections humans caught. There was, however, a variety of vampire flu I'd occasionally encountered.

Beatrice's forehead was as cool as your produce drawer—a healthy temperature. When a vampire has a fever, she's a little warmer than room temperature.

"You're right," I said. "You don't feel like you have a fever."

I checked the other three women, and they were all cool to the touch.

"I'll need to test you girls for the vampire flu. Are you available tomorrow?"

There were no commercial PCR or other tests available for strains of the vampire flu. At times like this, my patients were lucky that this former home-health nurse was also a witch. I had designed a magic spell that could detect the flu with more accuracy than even the tests for humans could.

The four discussed their schedules for the next evening, which were surprisingly complex for retired women, between leisure activities, board meetings, hair appointments, and water aerobics. Finally, they agreed this hour was fine with them.

I said my goodbyes and went in search of Agnes. I already had too much on my plate, but the women's complaints about fatigue worried me.

"I wonder if it's because of the mysterious creature we haven't been able to identify," I said to Agnes. I found her on a bench at the end of the dune crossover, gazing at the ocean in the moonlight.

"How could a creature cause this?" Agnes asked.

"I don't know, to be honest. It might be making them sick, just like a virus."

"If that's the case, we need to find it quickly."

⋯⋯⋯⋯

THE NEXT DAY, I wandered aimlessly down the aisles of the botanica, hoping to be inspired by something. I'd been at a loss for how to find the creature at Squid Tower that had been eluding me. None of my grimoires at home had a spell that could help me. Don Mateo was at a loss, too. Even Tony could offer nothing more than the assurance that some creature was, in fact, there.

I walked along the aisles. Could any of the saints, gods, and spirits represented by the statuettes in this store help? Would these potions for virility and success be of any help finding a mysterious organism?

The Santeria and voodoo statuettes were silent. I passed

the Christian saints in aisle two. They were silent, except for Saint Francis.

"You're such a disappointment," he said.

Yes, it was weird when an eight-inch-tall ceramic figurine, hand-painted rather sloppily, spoke to you. This wasn't the first time. He usually tried to make me feel guilty, which was odd because my adoptive parents didn't put a great deal of emphasis on religion when I was growing up.

My birth mother, who abandoned me when I was an infant, had supposedly been Catholic. My Catholic friends were overly susceptible to guilt, so it was conceivable that some latent Catholicism in my blood had egged on the ceramic St. Francis. And why was he enchanted? Because, well, this is the world I lived in.

"Why are you turning your back on nursing?" he asked. "You could help people. Instead, you mess around with all this infernal claptrap."

"I won't argue with you," I said, "but that ship has sailed."

I turned my back and walked away.

In the store's wing that I was setting up as a center for Old World witchcraft, I found no inspiration, either. Crystals, herbs, and pentagrams did not help.

"Why are you moping around?" Luisa asked me.

I explained my conundrum.

"Madame Tibodet is coming in today to counsel a client. Why don't you ask her for advice on finding the creature? She owes you a favor for rescuing Carl."

When the voodoo manbo arrived and headed for the back room, I sprang my questions on her.

"Oh, I wouldn't know anything about that," she said. She

wore a traditional floral Haitian dress and the headscarf she donned for her role as priestess. When off duty, she dressed like a typical American. Once, I saw her at the mall wearing designer duds.

"You would have to speak to my bokor, that nasty sorcerer," she continued. "He knows spells and hexes. All I can do is pray for a loa to help you, and they would only do that if they're in the mood."

"Where can I find your bokor?"

"You don't. He'll find you. I'll send a message to him for you."

Okay, so none of the various religions represented in this store would be of any help to me.

I scratched my head and pondered if science could help me. Perhaps, there were ways of testing for strange organisms.

As a medical professional who had long straddled the line between science and magic, I preferred magic.

⊲∘∘∘∘∘⊳

A "Mr. Bokor" sent me a text with a place and time to meet him later that day. I hadn't known what a bokor was until Madame Tibodet told me. She taught me the basics of the Caribbean-American varieties of voodoo and how they differed from their West African roots. I figured her bokor was a cross between a witch and a necromancer because he provided magical services and raised Carl from the dead.

I didn't expect him to have an office, though.

"Welcome to Jellyfish Beach Executive Center," the perky

receptionist said in a Southern drawl when Madame Tibodet and I got off the elevator. "How can I help y'all today?"

The executive center was one of those office-sharing spaces you'd use if you couldn't afford a corporate headquarters of your own. You rented a one-room office and shared a conference room and receptionist with the other tenants.

"We're here to see Mr. Bokor," Madame Tibodet said. She'd explained to me he refused to give his clients his actual name, insisting to go by his business name, which was 1-800-Mr-Bokor. His pickup truck stood out in the parking lot with its colorful logo for "1-800-Mr-Bokor Spiritual Services."

The receptionist told us to go on to Suite 304. We walked down the hall past a conference room and a tiny break room. Placards on the doors announced an accountant, an attorney, a medical-transcription service, and Mr. Bokor. Tendrils of incense smoke snaked from the bottom of his closed door.

I knocked.

"Enter," said a booming voice.

Yep, the guy was definitely a sorcerer. The office resembled the botanica, with its shelves of potions and bags of herbs and dried plants. He also had a large terrarium containing several snakes, which our shop did not—and would never—have.

A goat chewed contentedly on a book, and three chickens ran about. But what caught my eye was the cat with a monkey's head. The cat lay curled up on the desk, while its monkey head stared at me with an alarmed expression.

I shuddered at the sight of the cat-monkey chimera. Creating such creatures had nothing to do with voodoo, at least based on what I had learned about the religion.

Then, I remembered: Igor Stanisloopsky had a chimera in his mansion—a cat-dog.

"Hello. Do you, um, create chimeras yourself, Mr. Bokor?"

Madame Tibodet gave me an evil stare.

The cat-monkey screeched.

"I do. It's just a hobby."

"Is that a voodoo practice?"

"No," he said with a superior smile. "It's magic I developed on my own."

"Do you sell them as pets?"

"Only to the right homes. Are you interested?"

Yeah, the homes of the very wealthy like Igor, I thought, taking a quick photo of the creature for the Friends of Cryptids.

The monkey head glared at me.

"Um, no thanks."

"You are late for your appointment," Mr. Bokor said. He had strikingly dark skin and a shiny bald head. The middle-aged bokor was dressed business-casual like the accountant we had passed in his office down the hall.

"I'm sorry," Madame Tibodet said. "We had trouble parking. Your truck is taking up two spaces, and a herd of goats is taking up two more."

He shrugged. "What can I do for you?"

"How much would you charge to use your magic to locate a monster when we already know the community it's living in?"

His brow furrowed. "A monster?"

The cat-monkey screeched at me.

"Some kind of supernatural creature. It's probably very tiny, which is why we can't find it. It's currently hiding in a community of vampires on the beach." I assumed it was okay to talk about vampires with a guy who had a chimera in his office.

He slapped his desk. I jumped, and the monkey-cat hid behind a pile of boxes.

"I will never do business with vampires again! Ever!"

"Why?"

"A vampire hired me to hex another vampire and stiffed me on the bill."

My curiosity was fully aroused. "Tell me more."

"I hexed this vampire so he couldn't drink blood without getting sick. It was designed to make him starve to death with maximum suffering. The problem was, he became intolerant to only one blood type, so my client wouldn't pay the bill. Even after I gave a big discount."

Oh, my. It could be Hugh Humbert who was hexed.

"Can you give me your client's name?"

"No. That's against my ethics."

"What about the victim of the hex? Was it Hugh Humbert?"

"That is confidential."

"Did either vampire live in Squid Tower?"

"I can't say."

"You can try to kill someone, but it's somehow too unethical to give me any information?"

"Absolutely. Mr. Bokor has high standards."

"Okay. Did you sell a cat-dog to Igor Stanisloopsky?"

He slapped the desk again. "I told you I don't do business with vampires anymore!"

I tried additional coaxing, but it didn't work. I resorted to undignified begging. He remained adamant.

"At least tell me when you put the hex on the victim."

"It was over a year ago."

I sighed with exhaustion. "Thank you."

When we left, I caught the monkey head staring at me from behind a box. It growled.

If I understood correctly, Mr. Bokor's vampire client wanted to kill this unnamed vampire through starvation. That seemed extremely cruel, though it would be almost impossible to trace. When it didn't work, did the client finish the job with a stake in his heart?

And what was the motive? A lover's jealousy that he was cheating on her with humans? Doubtful, since it seemed Humbert only went out with human women, period. Or perhaps a male vampire loved the same human Humbert seduced?

I still felt investment fraud was the most likely motive. Assuming he wasn't killed by the Knights Simplar, the unlikeliness of which I reluctantly accepted.

◌◌◌◌◌◌◌◌

I CALLED Agnes with news of what Mr. Bokor had told me.

"He didn't tell you who his client was?" she asked.

"No, but you should free Courtney Peppers immediately."

"Why do you assume she isn't the vampire who paid for the hex?"

"Because a vampire ordered the hex, and it was performed several months before Courtney was turned. You need to let her go."

Agnes laughed ruefully. "If only it were that easy. The initial stages of the trial have already begun. You will need evidence more concrete than some sorcerer's word that he hexed Humbert for a vampire. That doesn't prove the vampire staked him."

"It shows someone tried to kill him. The hex simply wasn't effective enough."

"You might be on to something, Missy, but you need to find more evidence and an alternative culprit. The Policing Committee is not like a human court of law in which you have the assumption of innocence. Vampires would rather punish the innocent than let the guilty get away with crimes."

"The way things are going, you're punishing the innocent, and the guilty have no accountability."

"It seems you're the only one who can fix that, my dear."

"Yes, it does. When is the next hearing? I can't allow our client to go through it alone."

"Next Thursday. Humans are not allowed, but in your case, we'll make an exception."

CHAPTER 19

DETECTIVE SHORTLE COMES A-CALLING

My doorbell rang shortly after I called Agnes. I'd fed the cats but hadn't had time for anything else. When I answered the door, I must have been wearing a scowl.

It was Detective Cindy Shortle, in a crisp white Jellyfish Beach P.D. polo shirt, her long dark hair in a ponytail, her olive skin fresh and lustrous.

"Rough day?" she asked.

"You look delightful, too."

"I ask because I have a witness claiming you were responsible for vandalism and arson at a laundromat."

"Testimony, or you think you saw me in security footage, too?"

"The security cameras failed. We arrested two suspicious characters. One of them provided your name."

It had to have been Lord Arseton.

"You found him at the laundromat?"

"He was in the dryer. Permanent-press setting. The other individual was just standing there, allowing his associate to tumble dry. They appeared to be awakening from a drug-induced haze."

"Well, I wish to file a criminal complaint against *them*," I said, trying to get off the defensive. "Abduction and attempted murder of a local journalist, and abduction of a . . . another dude I know. We were rescuing the dude, who was locked in the van used by Mr. Permanent Press."

"Who was 'we'?"

"Me and the journalist we rescued earlier in the evening."

"You used 'we' again."

"I guess I did. Angela Davie helped me."

"The town librarian?"

I nodded, hoping it wasn't a mistake to bring Angela's name into this. I thought she would lend me more legitimacy.

"That sweet old lady helped you 'rescue' an abducted journalist? What is really going on here?"

I had to tread carefully as I improvised my way through a feasible explanation.

"The guy in the dryer—he was in there with tunics that had an embroidered eye on them, right?"

Shortle nodded, but her expression was skeptical.

"His name is Tim Tissy."

"He claimed it was Lord Arseton. What a dumb name. But his driver's license identified him as Timothy Tissy."

"He's a real nut job. He leads a cult, basically. They believe in witches and monsters and have a mission to kill them. They showed up at the botanica claiming that we attracted demons and such. So, they turned vigilante and abducted the dude I know. He's a customer of ours."

"What about the journalist?"

"He infiltrated the cult, so they abducted him, too, and tried to murder him."

"Tried? How?"

I described Matt's burial beside the river and the hungry alligators.

"Crazy! Who's the journalist you rescued?"

"Matt Rosen with *The Jellyfish Beach Journal*."

"Oh. That pain in the butt."

"The very same."

"Okay, so you claim you had nothing to do with the damage at the laundromat? Were you there at all?"

"We didn't go inside the laundromat," I lied. Sorry, but it was necessary. "We rescued the dude I know from the cultists' van in the parking lot." I figured my stretching of the truth was harmless. "It's obvious that Tissy and his goon were lying to you. They must have been all drugged-up when they vandalized the laundromat."

"I'll be the one who comes to conclusions," Shortle said, flaring her shoulders back.

"The dude I know who was abducted—his name is Carl Tibodet. He lives at his sister's house just south of downtown. She's a voodoo priestess named Madame Tibodet. Maybe, you'll find someone who witnessed the abduction. She might have security cameras on her property. You should speak to her. Carl probably won't be able to talk to you. Too traumatized."

"Thank you." She dropped her voice. "There's something else I need to ask you. May I come in?"

I opened the door wider and beckoned for her to enter. She followed me into the living room, scanning the room and hallway to make sure we were alone. Yep, I'm a solitary middle-aged witch. No one here but two cats and an iguana.

"Remember when I told you about the defiled doors of houses of worship?" She spoke as if we were childhood friends exchanging secrets.

I nodded.

"It's still happening, but it's more elaborate now than just cow dung. This is the Lutheran church on Second Street this morning." She opened her bag and withdrew a printed photo. "I'm showing you this because you're the only person I know who's into this kind of stuff."

"I'm not into church defilements." I didn't mind, though, if she knew me as an occult hobbyist. As long as she didn't discover I was a practicing witch with real magic.

The photo depicted a magical tableau of sorts on the concrete porch immediately in front of the heavy oaken doors. Miscellaneous objects were arrayed around a large black candle. There were bones, animal entrails, a bowl of what appeared to be blood, a vine with thorns, a bundle of herbs, and, yes, a pile of cow dung.

I immediately knew it didn't involve Santeria, voodoo, obeah, or any of the religions or rituals practiced by the botanica's customers. It didn't appear to be the work of the common types of witches.

It also didn't look like the product of bored teenagers, who I had originally suspected were behind the dung defilements.

"It looks evil," I said. "Something about it gives me the

chills. I know little about black magic, but if I had to guess, I'd say that's what's behind it."

"But what's the purpose? Simply to harass the houses of worship?"

"Has there been any other vandalism to the facilities?"

"Nothing has been reported."

My mind ran through the possibilities. "Have any of the clergy or congregants died or become ill?"

"I can say for sure that no one has been murdered. I'll need to inquire about illnesses or natural deaths."

"It could have been done as a warning. But I can't imagine what it's a warning of. This kind of thing will not stop people from worshipping. Do you mind if I borrow this photo?"

"No problem," Shortle said. "I have other copies."

"I'll ask around and let you know if I hear of any reasonable theories."

"As if reason had anything to do with this."

She thanked me and left.

Was I becoming the local occult consultant, as well as a monster cataloger?

I made a cup of tea and studied the photo of the church doorstep, grabbing a magnifying glass these middle-aged eyes needed more and more frequently.

Every item in the evil tableau appeared to be precisely placed with no randomness at all.

Then, I spotted it at the edge of the photo: a cigarette butt. It was unlikely to have been lying there before the items were placed in front of the door. This was a church, after all, not a bar.

I cast a simple spell upon the magnifying glass to enhance

its magnification. The image of the cigarette butt was pixelated from the zoom effect, but I could identify the brand of cigarette.

It was the brand my mother smoked.

⸎

YES, flicking on the garage's fluorescent light was a rude way to wake Tony. He lay atop a tree limb I had dragged into the space to serve as his sleeping perch. He was not pleased by the wake-up call.

"What the bleep do you think you're doin'? I was in the middle of an amorous dream."

"About a sexy iguana?"

"No. About Marilyn Monroe. Don't ask. Whatcha want in here? It's a late hour to be making one of your stinky potions." His reptilian foreleg gestured toward my workbench and propane stove.

"I'm here seeking your expertise." I showed him the photo. "What do you believe the purpose of this arrangement is in front of a church? I'm pretty sure it involves black magic."

His heavy-lidded eyes squinted at the photo.

"Who says I'm an expert on black magic?"

"You've been a witch's familiar for hundreds of years, as an iguana, a dog, and who knows what other creatures. I figured you'd have picked up some knowledge along the way."

"An aardvark."

"What?"

"One of my incarnations was as an aardvark. I hated being one, to be frank. But that's neither here nor there. I know enough to tell you this black-magic nonsense is their version of a warding spell. They don't use wards to protect like with white magic. They use 'em to harm or frighten."

"I don't understand the purpose of frightening worshippers away from their church. This junk was surely removed after the photo was taken, before anyone showed up for services. So, it would be pointless."

Tony shrugged. "Beats me."

"Allow me to examine the drawing," said the voice of Don Mateo.

He materialized beside us. No bras or panties came with him.

"I'm pleased to see you weren't in my lingerie drawer for once. Or were you?"

"I will not incriminate myself."

I held the photo in front of him. "It's a photo, not a drawing. Technology that came along centuries after you."

Don Mateo's apparition was solid enough that I could read the horror in his face.

"I know what these items are for." His voice was barely above a whisper. "A cult of heretics operated in Madrid back in my day. They fought the Spanish Inquisition using black magic. These are the materials for an imprisonment spell. It works on entities like me—ghosts, spirits, souls."

"How?"

"Those who attend this church will have their souls trapped inside the building."

"The people are trapped inside?"

"No, no. Their *souls* are. When the people leave, they leave without their souls."

"How can you survive without a soul?"

"You can't. Not for long. Unless another force replaces your soul. And something tells me it would be a force of evil."

I whipped out my phone and called Detective Shortle.

"Get word to all the houses of worship," I breathlessly said. "Tell them to beef up their security. If they see a display like this, tell them to remove it immediately. Under no circumstance should anyone go inside the building while this junk is in front of the door. And if anyone happens to be in the building when the stuff is placed outside, they must have someone else remove it before they leave the building."

"That's crazy. All because of the defilement?"

"Churches, temples, and mosques are meant to gather souls inside. We want to make sure the souls don't stay in there."

"You're making no sense."

"What I'm saying could very well be superstitious nonsense. But let's play it on the safe side, okay?"

I couldn't help wondering why my mother would be involved with this scheme. Perhaps, the brand of cigarette in the crime-scene photo was just a coincidence. Perhaps, it was the brand all the black-magic sorcerers smoked.

Oh, my.

CHAPTER 20

COMMITTEE CONUNDRUM

The beauty of using magic for a flu test was that very little mess or danger was involved. No swabbing, no getting too close to jaws and fangs. And since vampires couldn't go to regular doctors, there was no need to use a medical-association-approved test.

If my patients needed prescriptions for human medications, I still had my nurse-practitioner's license and could write them myself. Most likely, though, I would treat their flu with a good dose of magic.

Beatrice, Henrietta, Gladys, and Gloria each had to spit into their own bowl filled with my proprietary potion.

"I don't want to spit in front of the others," Beatrice complained.

"Then take the bowl into the bathroom," I suggested.

"And you know that vampires have very little saliva."

"Yes, I do. All we need is a tiny amount. So please, stop making this difficult. The test is hardly invasive."

After assorted moans and clucks of disapproval, all four of the vampires complied with my instructions. I placed the four bowls inside a magic circle, gathered my energies, and went through the ritual.

I waited.

A positive result would turn the potion black before creating a small explosion. I braced myself. Nothing happened.

"Ladies, I'm pleased to announce that none of you has the vampire flu."

"Then, what's making me feel so run-down?" Gladys asked with a whine.

Good question.

"I'VE BEGUN to believe the fact that we haven't been able to find the creature—or creatures—suggests that it is a microbe too small for human or vampire eyes to see," I said to Agnes on the terrace, or moon deck, as the vampires called it, right after the negative tests. "There's another possibility, though. What if it's hiding in plain sight?"

"What do you mean?"

"What if it's one of us?"

"Can witches drain vitality like this?"

"Evil ones, yes. Can vampires?"

Agnes stroked her chin in thought.

"I'm the longest-existing vampire in this community," she said. "But I'm not an expert on the undead. We need to speak with Sol. He's somewhat of a scholar on the history of vampirism."

Agnes made a phone call, and almost instantly, Sol showed up on the terrace with us.

"Do you know of any vampires that can cause enervation in other vampires?" Agnes asked him.

"Haven't you heard of psychic vampires?" Sol asked. The moonlight shined on the white skin of his bald head and pointy ears, enhancing his resemblance to Nosferatu.

"The term sounds vaguely familiar."

"Yes, they feed on psychic energy instead of blood. Sometimes, that can have a physical effect on the victim, like you're anemic or simply exhausted."

"Would a psychic vampire feed on other vampires?" I asked.

"I would hope not, but you never know."

"How can you recognize a psychic vampire?" Agnes asked.

"You can't, really. They would have to admit they're one."

"Before you guys start looking at everyone with suspicion, let me make sure it's not an ailment other than the flu," I said. "What's that expression about the simplest explanation being the correct one?"

"Oh, but nothing is simple with the vampires in Squid Tower," Agnes said.

"I'm trying to find an answer for you," I said. "I truly am."

Frankly, I had more pressing priorities now than diagnosing run-down vampires.

◦◖◗◖◗◖◗◖◗◘◦

HER TIME IN CONFINEMENT, without her regular tanning-bed sessions, had left Courtney as pale as death. Which meant she looked like a healthy vampire. But the stress showed in the lines around her mouth and eyes. She told me they fed her fresh blood every night from the Blood Bus, but being confined in the condo gave her too much time to worry about her predicament. I patted her ice-cold hand as we sat side-by-side on the folding chairs facing a long table in the community room.

At first glance, the room looked like a meeting of the HOA board was going on. However, instead of debating landscaping contracts, the solemn vampires seated at the table were deciding whether Courtney should permanently die.

"The human has petitioned the committee to say a word on her client's behalf," Leonard Schwartz said, annoying me. He knew my name; why refer to me that way?

I stood and approached the table. Schwartz, Agnes, Beatrice, Beverly, and Oleg stared back with neutral expressions. Beatrice's face was decidedly hostile. She was on the committee because she and her husband owned more units than anyone else at Squid Tower. They lived in one and rented the others to newly made vampires and those who were coming to Florida for the first time. Walt, I believed, was renting from them. I heard Beatrice demanded exorbitant rents.

"Thank you for allowing me to speak tonight," I said. Next, I reviewed the facts I believed exonerated Courtney.

I explained it made little sense for her to hire me to intervene with Humbert if she was going to stake him. Humbert's defrauding of his clients was extensive and egregious, which would create the true culprit's motive. Furthermore, the fact that Humbert's laptop had been stolen from us added credence to this. Finally, I repeated what Mr. Bokor had told me about the hex being commissioned by a vampire.

I thanked the committee and sat down.

"That all sounds very reasonable to me," Agnes said. "I move that we delay the trial until more evidence can be collected."

"Evidence, schmevidence," Schwartz said. "We should decide this the old-fashioned vampire way: trial by combat."

Courtney gasped. Oleg smiled and nodded. Beatrice perked up.

"I like that idea," she said. "The old ways are more dependable."

"Nonsense," Agnes said. "The old ways were barbaric."

"They were entertaining to watch."

"Ridiculous," Agnes said. "Who would fight her? You, Beatrice? Or you, Leo?"

Schwartz patted his pot belly absently. "Not me. I figured we'd bring in a vampire who's the same body age as the defendant."

Agnes moved so quickly my eyes didn't register it. The diminutive elderly vampire stood on the table, holding Schwartz aloft by his neck. His legs twitched as he dangled above his knocked-over chair.

"If you believe the old ways are 'entertaining,' you're mistaken," Agnes said, her fangs fully extended. "With the old ways, if I disagreed with you, I could simply pop your head off. As the president of the HOA, I am the leader of this nest and have the right to do so. Shall I pop his head off?"

"I won't stop you," Oleg said.

Schwartz gurgled in protest.

I had to admit I found it mildly entertaining to watch a bully like Schwartz get a taste of his own medicine, but I did not want Agnes to pop his head off.

Agnes released his neck, and Schwartz dropped to the floor atop his fallen chair.

"I don't care how many centuries any of you have lived," Agnes said, still standing on the table. "We are in the twenty-first century now. To make our existences safe and simple, we must dress in the current fashions, speak in the current lingo, and conduct ourselves according to the current jurisprudence. That means no trial by combat, and no executing innocent vampires. As the chairperson of this committee, and the leader of this community, I rule that we postpone the trial for one week while Missy gathers more evidence for her client."

"Only one week?" I asked.

The way Agnes glared at me told me the matter was settled. I didn't want to be dangling by my neck.

⊗〔⊃⊃⊃⊃〕⊗

I WAS FRUSTRATED that Mr. Bokor hadn't told me who hired him to hex Humbert. My truth-telling spell probably wouldn't work on a sorcerer, so I didn't know how to get the information short of breaking into his office. That would be my last resort.

Then again, might the vampire who ordered the hex on Humbert *not* be the one who staked him? It was possible, considering that Humbert had defrauded so many clients. I wished I had been able to go through Humbert's laptop for more information.

The only solution I could think of was to find a backup of the stolen laptop's data. Sal did the best he could to search for a site in the cloud, but without the laptop, he could only search using the I.P. address he had found before. He came up empty.

The only other hope would be to find an external hard drive. That meant I had to return to Humbert's condo. Which meant Agnes had to let me in. She was not happy about my request.

"Pardon my impertinence," I said when I called her, "but you've seemed a bit cranky lately."

Specifically, I had in mind the image of Schwartz in her death grip. And her tone when she answered the phone.

"Me, cranky? I have a creature draining the energy from all the residents. *And* I must preside over the execution of a vampire. Why would I be cranky?"

"You don't have to execute her. She's innocent."

"I'm not confident in your ability to prove otherwise, Missy. That's why I gave you only a week to do so. I have a nest of homeowners who have been pressuring me to exact retribution on our prisoner."

"But she's innocent."

"I know you believe so, dear. But you'd have to convince the committee of that, and it doesn't appear you can, no matter how much time we give you. If I don't deliver justice, they will hold a no-confidence vote on me, and I will lose."

"Being an HOA president is a lot of work," I said. "Wouldn't you enjoy more free time?"

"When the leader of a nest receives a no-confidence vote, they're usually put to the stake."

"Oh. Isn't that harsh?"

"Welcome to the world of vampires."

"It's even more reason to let me into Humbert's condo again."

"I never said I wouldn't. Only that I doubted you would find anything. Come on, then. Let us get this over with."

We took the elevator down two floors, and Agnes let me into Humbert's condo with the spare key all residents must leave at the office.

When she opened the door, I was shocked at the sight. The condo had been ransacked.

CHAPTER 21

DEGENERATE DISCOVERIES

"Oh, my," I said.

Agnes muttered an ancient Visigoth curse word. I've heard her use it before and never asked her to translate, because I got the gist simply from the sound of it.

The trespasser hadn't dumped the contents of drawers on the floor, but all had been rummaged through. Cabinets and closets were left open. Sofa cushions were pushed aside. In the bedroom, the wooden platform for the punctured waterbed had been knocked off its supports.

"They were quite thorough," Agnes said.

"Which might mean they didn't find what they were looking for. If the hard drive is still here, I don't know."

I explained to Agnes that Humbert might have had thumb drives—some call them USB sticks—but they don't have the memory capacity to back up his entire computer and the financial services database. Aside from the cloud, only an external hard drive would have enough memory for that. Nowadays, they could be as small as the palm of your hand. Still, someone who tore apart the condo like this should have found an object of that size.

I glanced into the half-open drawers and cabinets in each room, particularly the ones that held random junk. Hopefully, Humbert's drive looked unusual, causing the searcher to miss it. But I didn't find anything.

"Do you have any spells that can help you find this drive?" Agnes asked.

"Let me think. My usual locating spells wouldn't work in this case."

Before I resorted to magic, I would use a bit of logic. To make backing up worthwhile, you needed to do it regularly, so if your computer died, you would only lose the most recent data. Humbert would keep the drive somewhere convenient, not, for instance, in a bank safe-deposit box, unless he had something he wanted to hide. He'd left his laptop sitting on his desk, so he wasn't concerned about what was on it.

I tried to think of a scenario in which what the thief was looking for wasn't on the stolen laptop when they searched it. Or were they looking for the hard drive simply to keep someone else from finding it?

If Humbert had info that was dangerous or legally perilous, he would have deleted it, right?

Unless he was using it to blackmail someone.

But that could be anything: photos, videos, proof of financial crimes. My original theory that the culprit was a victim of Humbert's financial fraud still made the most sense.

To devise a spell that could help me find the hard drive, I

needed to imagine if Humbert intended to conceal the drive or merely place it in a safe but easy-to-access spot.

Well, there's a spell for that. A simple one.

If you're doing a routine activity, such as backing up your computer and putting the backup drive somewhere safe, you barely think about it. You certainly feel little emotion.

The opposite is true if you're being furtive and trying to conceal something. Your emotions are intense. You could experience guilt, shame, resentment, or greed. You could gloat about something you have that you don't want others to know about or find. There's often anxiety mixed in—a fear of being discovered.

Such powerful emotions create energy that tends to linger. My spell allows me to detect it.

I explained to Agnes what I was going to do. She nodded and sat on an undamaged chair in the living room.

My usual ritual of spellcasting wouldn't be possible here, without my paraphernalia. The fact is, many of the rituals I use are more about their effect on my mind and mood, rather than directly creating magic. The magic I needed was always within me. It was just a matter of coaxing it out.

My one crutch was the power charm I always carried in my pocket. It actually did contain magic, which amplified my own.

Clutching the charm, I cleared my mind and went into a meditative state. I visualized the energies in my core, focused on them, and drew them together in a tight ball. After reciting a brief incantation I had memorized years ago, I released the energies and activated the spell.

It created a cloud of magic around me that followed me

wherever I went. The cloud was invisible to everyone except me. What I saw was a sparkling haze.

I walked through every square foot of Humbert's two-bedroom, two-bath, oceanfront condo. Whenever I encountered the lingering energy of emotion, it lit up the sparkling cloud.

Most of the emotions I found were of the everyday sort: brief physical and mental pleasures or frustrations.

In Humbert's office, he left minor feelings of guilt, probably related to his financial scamming. It wasn't until I entered his bedroom that my magic cloud lit up like a lightning storm at night.

I already knew about Humbert's escapades with human women, so I steered clear of the emptied waterbed mattress where the naughty emotions were strongest. But as I passed by his nightstand, my cloud lit up again with different emotions. The furtive kind.

Yes, there was a mixture of sneakiness, guilt, anxiety about getting caught, and secret pleasure. Very odd. What was setting off these emotions?

I looked through the nightstand's drawer. It was empty except for a book about cryptocurrency and a sex toy. In a vase was an orchid with three beautiful flowers. The plant looked fake. I touched the flower petals to make sure, and that was when I found it.

The stamen of one flower was a tiny surveillance camera aimed at the bed. I pulled the plant from the pot, and at its base was a tiny black box that contained a micro battery and a camera memory card.

Humbert had been taking secret videos of his activities in bed.

My mind reeled as I assessed what this meant. My theory that he was staked by a fraud victim could be wrong. Perhaps, he had been using videos of a lover to blackmail her, threatening to send them to a husband or boyfriend, or posting them publicly.

That meant Courtney could have been his murderer. Or Lisa Alvarez. Or potentially dozens of girlfriends he met through online dating apps that I didn't know about.

I thought about it more and found a flaw in my logic. If any of his lovers had seen the videos they were in, and they had broken into his condo, they would have looked for a camera in his bedroom. The fake orchid was positioned in such a way that they'd likely have at least noticed it and found the tiny camera, and thus the memory card. And taken them both. Even if they hadn't found the actual camera, wouldn't they have torn apart the condo looking for a backup drive?

I glanced around the bedroom, atop the dresser and the other nightstand. Could there have been another camera, placed somewhere else, that the searcher found?

My memory supplied me with an image. When I had glanced into the spaces the intruder had already searched, I had found a bunch of fake plants and flowers under the sink. At the time, I thought nothing of it.

I rushed out to the kitchen. As I knelt in front of the sink, my cloud sparkled with the same furtive, guilty emotions I had found in the bedroom.

I opened the cabinet door and found the fake plants. One by one, I took them out and examined them. All had cameras hidden in fake flower blossoms, or inside fake stems, stalks, and branches. Each one had a small black box at the bottom of the pot, usually covered with moss or mulch.

Also beneath the sink was an unlabeled cardboard box, slightly smaller than a shoebox. It contained several more cameras disguised as twigs, flowers, or leaves that could be placed in actual flowerpots. These appeared to be designed to connect with Wi-Fi.

Regardless of whether the videos were captured on a memory card or transmitted via Wi-Fi, they had to end up on a computer to be viewed.

"Wow," I said aloud.

"What did you find?" Agnes asked.

I explained to her how the murder case had taken an unexpected, complicated turn. It took a great deal of explaining. Even though Agnes was in touch with technology much more than your typical 1,500-year-old, the video voyeurism was new to her.

"It's become a big problem now at vacation rentals," I explained.

"Oh, no," she said. "I just remembered something. After Humbert started losing all his investment clients, he started taking on odd jobs for extra cash. That included electrical work and painting in the condos that Beatrice and her husband rent out."

That sent my mind reeling again. Too much mind reeling can leave you feeling dizzy.

"Humbert must have placed cameras in those units," I said. "He probably had compromising videos of the tenants, not just of him and his girlfriends. He could have been blackmailing any or all those tenants, men or women."

"Many of Beatrice's rentals are short-term, just for the season or until the vampires decide where they want to buy. I can't imagine how many vampires he could have filmed."

"So, the intruder *was* searching for an external hard drive. They stole the laptop and later realized the videos could be backed up somewhere else."

"Or a different victim stole the laptop than the one looking for the hard drive," Agnes said.

My heart sank when I thought about how complicated it would be to find the murderer. If multiple people and vampires were blackmailed, how could I prove who staked Humbert and rule out Courtney?

"We must find the videos," I said. "It's the only way we can find out who has been compromised. I'll check the memory cards of all these cameras, but there could be countless more videos on the hard drive."

I searched the condo again, with Agnes helping me. There was no hard drive.

"What if he didn't back up the videos?" Agnes asked. "He kept only one copy on his computer, and after his victims paid him off, he deleted the videos as promised."

I looked at her with one eyebrow cocked.

"Yes, you're right," she said. "He's the kind of person who would keep a copy for himself."

I gathered the memory cards from all the cameras and left, dreading what I would find on them.

THE NEXT MORNING, I went to a nearby computer store and bought an SD card reader so I could transfer the images to my computer. I steeled myself for what I was going to see.

It turned out that the cards from the cameras under the sink were all blank. The one from the orchid in his bedroom had one video with a bit of spice with a woman I didn't recognize, who appeared to be human. Her face wasn't clear, and the lighting was bad. I doubted the video would be blackmail worthy.

After sunset, I called Agnes.

"We need to speak with Beatrice," I said. "Did she know what Humbert was up to? And even if she didn't, we need to remove any cameras that are in her properties."

"After the Blood Bus arrives, we're playing bridge. Come by at eleven."

Great, I thought. Another night of vampire hours to mess with my internal clock.

After parking in the Squid Tower visitors' lot, I walked past the parking garage toward the lobby, then stopped. I wondered if Humbert's car was still there and if whoever was looking for the hard drive had broken into it.

Now, you might wonder why a human would willingly walk into a dark parking garage filled with cars owned by vampires. And by dark, I mean pitch black. Vampires don't need lighting in there, so why waste the money?

But I had to know.

Using the light on my smartphone, I located the spot for

Humbert's unit. An old Mercedes that had seen better days sat there with no signs of forced entry. It was locked, of course. Peering inside, I saw nothing of interest, just a sweater and some golf shoes. I was late for my appointment and hurried into the building, hoping the women were still in the card room.

The other bridge partners had left, and only Agnes and Beatrice were there, speaking in low tones. Beatrice frowned when she saw me.

"Beatrice says she knew nothing about Hugh's cameras," Agnes announced.

"I lent him the keys, and he worked in the units without supervision," Beatrice said. "I inspected his work afterward and saw no cameras."

"They're designed not to be seen."

Beatrice remained skeptical.

"Can we check the units?" I asked.

"No. They're occupied by tenants. All but one."

"Let's check it out. If we find a camera, you must notify your tenants about this."

She got up with a huff, and I followed her down the hall to the condominium office. I was surprised to see her use a key from her keychain to open the glass case that held duplicate keys to all the units in the building, stored here in case of an emergency. I looked at Agnes with quirked eyebrows, but she seemed fine with it. Beatrice removed the keys that belonged to the vacant rental condo.

"The spare keys to the units I own are upstairs in my condo," she explained. "This will save us time."

Next, we took the elevator to the second floor. The condo was a three-bedroom, two-bath, and was furnished.

"The couple who rented this last bought a unit on a higher floor," Beatrice said.

Having already seen Humbert's arsenal of spare cameras, I knew what to look for.

All the plants and flowers in the condo were fake, which is a good idea for vampire living spaces that receive no natural light.

In the space of five minutes, I found three cameras. One was in an orchid facing the living room sofa. Another was embedded in a cactus in the master bath. And the third was in a potted hibiscus with a perfect view of the master bedroom's king bed.

Beatrice looked shaken. "I had no idea."

I slipped the memory card out of each device without her noticing. I didn't want her to prevent me from viewing the footage out of some faux concern for her tenants' privacy.

I suspected video voyeurism was a crime, and I would probably break the law by viewing the footage. But we were not in the realm of human law. This was Vampire Land, where they could execute someone based on the decisions of a handful of HOA board members. So, excuse me for bending the rules.

Beatrice did a bunch of tut-tutting about how terrible this was. She promised to inform her current tenants to look for cameras—which I doubted she would do, in fear of being held liable for the invasion of privacy.

At one point, I managed to separate Agnes from her.

"I need to return to Humbert's condo to look for his car keys," I said.

Agnes had an eureka expression. "Of course! Why didn't we think to look in his car?"

"I've always been told to never leave valuable electronics in my car. But it would make sense for him to store it there—not in his condo, but easily accessible to allow regular backups."

"Can't your magic unlock his car?"

"Yeah, but it's not easy. Let's look for the keys first."

We entered Humbert's condo, and we both searched the normal places people stored their car keys: the bowl on the small table near the front door, the bowl on the kitchen counter, the bowl on top of the dresser in his bedroom. Then, we looked in just about every drawer in most of the rooms.

I had an insight: Humbert was a guy. So, I searched the floor until I found a pair of crumpled trousers half under the bed. In the left pocket was the key fob for a Mercedes. Of course.

Before we went to the parking garage, I retrieved a flash-light from my car. As a human investigating in the vampires' world, I was at a distinct disadvantage when it came to eyesight.

When it came to intelligence, I was determined to prove I was, at least, their equal.

CHAPTER 22
VAMPIRE BYTES

Agnes watched me dubiously as I opened the glove compartment, peered into the center console box, and felt inside the driver's door storage trough.

"You've got to check the obvious spots first," I said, smiling sheepishly at Agnes.

I moved to the passenger seat, then the back seats, searching all the storage bins, reaching beneath seats, even looking inside Humbert's golf shoes.

One thing you could say about the vampire: he kept a clean car.

Now, all my hope was resting in the trunk. I popped it open and was disappointed to find only an umbrella and roadside emergency kit.

"No more obvious places left," I said.

"His car itself is too obvious a place to store the drive," Agnes said. "Don't you think he'd find someplace cleverer?"

"Yeah. But you have to weigh cleverness against convenience. A backup drive is worthless if it's too inconvenient to use. Let me try my emotion-sensing spell to see if he had a clever hidey-hole."

Agnes remained quiet while I concentrated on creating the spell. This time, I could do it faster. In the darkness of the garage, I couldn't see the cloud surrounding me, but the sparkles stood out like fireflies.

Back in the car's cabin were traces of the unremarkable emotions we all would feel while running errands. I touched the steering wheel. This was the first time I vicariously felt the emotion of stalking prey. But I couldn't get over the fact he would do it from his car. How lazy was that?

I opened the hood but didn't feel any emotion at all under there.

When I returned to the trunk, that's when the furtive, sneaky emotions appeared, sparks flying through the cloud surrounding me. Among them was a feeling of pride.

"I think I found his cleverness," I said.

Somewhere in here must be a secret compartment. I pulled up the mat and removed the spare tire. There were no secret openings or crevices here. I shined my flashlight and ran my other hand over every surface inside the trunk, along the floor, the inside of the lid, and the sides. There were small spaces inside the framing on either side, but they were empty.

It looked like my hunch was a bust.

When I picked up the spare tire to return it, it felt strangely lightweight. It was one of those temporary spares, but it should have been heavier than this. The tire wasn't firm; in fact, it felt like there was no air in it at all. Interesting.

I studied it closely under the beam of the flashlight. And

there it was: on the inner side of the tire, next to the rim, was a rectangular slit in the rubber. I forced a finger through the slit and pulled open the little rubber door.

Inside the deflated tire was a backup drive, about the size of a pack of cigarettes, held in place with Velcro.

I cackled with triumph before announcing my discovery to Agnes.

"I was right," she said. "This is a clever place to hide it."

I removed the drive and stuffed it in my pocket. After returning the tire, closing the trunk, and locking the car, I handed the key fob to Agnes.

"Can you please return this to his condo? I'm eager to get home and search this drive. If it contains everything I hope it does, I have a lot of work ahead of me."

꘎꘎꘎

I SUCCESSFULLY CONNECTED and mounted the external drive to my computer. The good news was this drive was the Holy Grail backup I'd hoped to find. The bad news was there were several terabytes of videos and financial information on it.

I know you're dying to know about the videos, so I'll get right to the point. I won't describe what Humbert filmed in his bedroom, because it was the expected footage of him carrying on with his much younger human girlfriends.

The footage from Beatrice's rental condos was excruciatingly dull. It was unedited, triggered by motion, and usually showed only someone walking past the camera and doing boring stuff.

Buried among all these banal videos was the prize. The tenant of one condo was a handsome male vampire with a body age of late fifties. The suave, dark-haired gentleman liked to entertain lady vampires in his bedroom, one in particular who was older than he.

One who I recognized quite easily, despite her performing naughty contortions.

The woman vampire was Beatrice.

Who, I should remind you, was married. Making her a perfect target for blackmail.

I had no proof yet that Humbert blackmailed her. I needed to delve more deeply into her relationship with him. Namely, was she a client, despite her denials of having invested with him?

Entering the username and password Sal had given me before, I accessed Humbert's financial-planning software. It was an ocean of information that I feared would drown me.

The first thing I did was search to see if Beatrice had an account with him. Sure enough, she did. I pulled it up and scrolled through the numbers.

Wow, she had nearly thirty million dollars with Humbert. Matt could help me look for signs of fraud if I couldn't spot them myself.

What I found was the account had been closed by Humbert, with the entire balance transferred to her bank. On her page were links to various documents and correspondence, and the second-to-last document was from Beatrice. It was a request to close the account based on a complaint about Humbert's mismanagement. Not fraud—incompetence.

It didn't appear that he had stolen from her. It looked like she got all her money back. No reason to stake him for fraud.

However, with her withdrawal of her funds, Humbert lost the large management fees he'd been charging on her thirty-million-dollar balance. At that time, his business was crumbling around him, which was when he'd started working as a handyman for Beatrice to make ends meet.

He might have deemed blackmail to be a better source of income, especially since he possessed spicy videos of Beatrice, which he could threaten to send to her husband.

I needed evidence that he had threatened her. Good luck with that. Sal would have to hack into Humbert's email account, but if Humbert was smart, he wouldn't have saved any blackmail notes. He probably only threatened her verbally, anyway. I also wished Sal could hack into Humbert's personal bank account so I could see if there were checks or money transfers coming from Beatrice.

Scrolling through Humbert's client database, I wondered if he had his own investment account with his company. I mean, why not?

I searched for his name, and bingo!

To my untrained eye, his investments weren't doing so well. Yet, there were regular withdrawals, steadily lowering the total of his holdings.

The only transfer of money into his account occurred a few days before he was staked. I wrote down the account number the money had come from. Then, I returned to Beatrice's page. The bank account that was linked to her investment account had the same number as the one that wired money to Humbert.

Yep, to these untrained eyes, it looked like Beatrice had made her first and only blackmail payment to Humbert.

If he had dared to ask for more, it could have been enough to push Beatrice over the edge.

And send her to a sporting-goods store to buy the fishing spear we found impaled in his waterbed mattress.

Since Matt had worked on stories involving financial fraud, I invited him over so I could bounce my theories off him.

"You saw the videos of her cheating on her husband with the renter?" he asked while he sipped a beer.

"I saw snippets of it. That was all I could stomach."

"Do you know her husband?"

"I've met him, but don't know him personally. This is a second marriage for both of them. They met and were married after being turned. I heard it was a lovely ceremony in a grave-yard. Anyway, he's older than she is, like several hundred years older. And he's very traditional—not the kind of guy who would take kindly to his wife cheating on him."

"Meaning, she would have a big incentive to keep it secret."

"You've got that right."

"Well, the evidence you have might not be enough to put a human behind bars, but it's probably enough to convince the Policing Committee to take a really close look at Beatrice."

"I hope so, because she's pushing to execute my client as soon as possible."

"Wow. That's scary. She's going to get an innocent person executed to cover up her own crime."

"Exactly."

"Missy, you better not confront Beatrice about this."

"Who, me?"

"Yes. I know you too well. This is vampire business. Don't take it personally. Let them sort it out."

"They want to execute my client."

"Not after they see your evidence."

"Don't be so sure about that."

CHAPTER 23

COUSINS FROM NEW JERSEY

M att backed up the hard drive onto the new one he brought.

"Since the vampire ninja is so good at stealing, we can't be too safe," he said. "I'll bring this home and lock it inside my desk. Be careful with the original drive. Even though we have a copy now, these drives can easily fail."

Not long after Matt left, two middle-aged thuggish vampires showed up at my house and rang the doorbell. I was being summoned to appear before the Policing Committee. They wore the uniforms of the vampire-owned security service Squid Tower used to man the entrance gate, but I'd never seen them before.

"You must come with us now," said the shorter, beefier one.

"Now?"

"And you will bring the computer hard drive you found last night, the one that belonged to the deceased Hugh Humbert. And the camera from his bedroom."

"Why?"

"They have evidence on them."

Agnes was the only vampire who knew I had found the drive, though I hadn't had the chance to let her know what was on it. She must have innocently mentioned my find to Beatrice. I was in for a world of hurt.

I had to assume Beatrice was the one who stole the laptop and searched Humbert's condo for the hard drive. If she got her hands on it, she would destroy it, wiping out all the data that tied her to Humbert and his blackmail scheme.

The thugs were visibly put off by my vampire-repelling amulets, but that wasn't enough. I needed to keep them out of my home.

"What kind of evidence?" I asked, trying to delay while I formed a quick warding spell to block my front door.

"Legal evidence," the taller vampire said. "This is important. Vampires were murdered."

These two thugs were a reminder that when you turn brutish humans, you get brutish vampires—not smarter than when they were human, but much more lethal.

"I'll get the stuff you want," I said, "if you two will wait on the porch."

The short one tried to walk inside but stopped when he hit an invisible wall.

"They warned us you're a witch," he said. "Don't think we can't get in there."

I did think it. A full protection spell would keep them out, but they would probably awaken neighbors with their buffoonish attempts to find a way inside. Besides, I didn't want to be besieged in my home every night. This tale must be brought to its conclusion.

"I'll be right back," I said, heading for my bedroom.

I picked up the cardboard box that held the cameras and memory cards. But I didn't put the hard drive in it. Instead, I slipped it under my mattress.

"Sorry, guys," I said to Brenda and Bubba, who'd been hiding under the bed ever since the doorbell rang.

Inside my closet, on the top shelf, sat some unneeded computer junk. I found an old backup drive and tossed it in the box. It didn't look at all like Humbert's, but it would fool Beatrice. At least, until she examined it. I grabbed the box, broke the warding spell, and joined the thugs on my front porch.

"Let's go," I said.

The two vampires led me to their black SUV, keeping their distance because of my amulets. Their body language made it clear, though, that I was in their custody.

At Squid Tower, the SUV pulled right up to the front door, and the vampires ushered me into the community room. Agnes, Schwartz, Beverly, Oleg, and Beatrice watched me closely, the latter with a manic gleam in her eyes.

"I apologize for bringing you here without notice," Agnes said to me. "When I reported to the others about the video voyeurism, they wanted to resolve this right away."

I nodded curtly. The truth was, I wish she'd kept her mouth shut until I fully examined the data and created a plan for dealing with Beatrice. This was a little awkward right now.

"It sounds like we now have an obvious motive for why the defendant staked Humbert," Beatrice said. "He had sex tapes of her and threatened to reveal them."

"I didn't see any footage of Courtney," I said. "At least none in which you can see her face and identify her."

"I'm certain it exists. The camera was pointed at the bed."

"If you don't believe me, we can watch the footage together," I bluffed.

"That won't be necessary," Beatrice snapped. "I motion we vote for execution."

"There's a laptop on the table. We can watch the footage right now."

"I don't want to look at smut," Agnes said.

"Maybe we should," Schwartz said a little too eagerly. "Perform our due diligence and all."

"It's not appropriate during a hearing," Beatrice snapped.

"We should look at the footage from his other two cameras, as well," I said. "Including the scenes of Beatrice and her renter in three-twelve."

Agnes gasped. Schwartz barked a nervous laugh. Beatrice growled.

"Stop talking nonsense," she said with false bravado.

"Yes, there are some... shall I say quite acrobatic performances of Beatrice in action. You would never believe this sweet, timid lady could be so ferocious. Her husband would be equally shocked to see it."

"Stop your lies! And get out of this room now!"

"In fact, Humbert threatened to send the videos to your husband unless you paid him, didn't he? That was after you shut down your investment account with him, and he was desperate for money. You made one payment, though. I assume he wanted more. That was why you paid the voodoo bokor to hex him and make him incapable of digesting blood so he would starve to death. But the hex didn't work completely."

"Get out of this room!"

"Then, you staked him. You knew I would hack into his laptop, so you stole it from me. You searched his condo in case he had a backup drive, but you couldn't find it. Unfortunately for you, I found it."

Beatrice leaped from her chair and grabbed my external hard drive from the box. She threw it with preternatural vampire strength. Instead of smashing against the wall, it punched right through into the card room next door.

"Ouch!" a male screamed from the card room. "I'm going to sue you!"

"That's not the drive," I said. "You're trying to execute an innocent vampire just to cover up your own crime. You're pathetic."

"This is meshuga," Schwartz said. "We need to clear this up."

"I refuse to vote for execution," Agnes said. "The vote has to be unanimous to pass."

"The human is lying," Beatrice insisted. "How can you believe a word a human says?"

"We must see your evidence," Schwartz said to me.

"You just want to look at smut," Beatrice said. "I'm sending these guards back to the witch's house to get the actual drive."

"I didn't bring it here because you'll destroy it."

"No, she won't," Agnes said. "I'm the presiding member of the committee. I want to examine and judge the evidence myself. Bring the drive directly to me," she ordered the guards.

I WAS A PRISONER, but presumably would be freed after delivering the hard drive to Agnes, right? Please? The thugs hadn't taken my phone, so I texted Matt.

They're taking the hard drive. Be vigilant.

Vampires can't read minds, as far as I knew, but it seemed reckless to mention in any way the existence of the duplicated drive. I hoped Matt understood my implications.

"Who are you texting?" the shorter thug, who was riding shotgun, asked.

"A coworker about a shipment." I didn't care if he believed me.

"Garth, you forgot your headlights again," said the thug.

"Silly me. Wish I didn't have to use them," the tall one said, clicking on the lights. He wore dark shades to protect his eyes against the oncoming headlights.

When we arrived at my house, my escorts came inside with me, even following me to my bedroom.

"Don't be rude," I said, reaching down and plucking the hard drive from under my mattress.

The tall thug, Garth, snatched it from my hand so quickly, I barely saw the movement.

"Beatrice said you probably made a copy of it. Where is it?"

He stared into my eyes so intently it startled me.

"What? I didn't make a copy."

"You made a copy. Tell me where it is."

His voice had a hypnotic quality. His words poured into me like water, filling my brain, making it mushy.

Oh, my. He's mesmerizing me. I should have prepared a spell to protect myself. It was too late now—my thoughts were sluggish, and my will was weak.

"Tell me where the copy is."

I tried to walk away from him, but my legs wouldn't obey me.

"Tell me where the copy is. You'll feel much happier when you do. Tell me. You *want* to tell me."

Being a witch requires immense self-control and powers of concentration. Forming magic out of thin air using the elemental energies and magic within you also requires faith in yourself.

Mine had completely drained away as my mind filled with his mesmerizing.

"I don't know." I fought as hard as I could, but I was fading.

"She's a tough nut to crack," the short thug muttered.

"Tell me where the copy is," Garth said, his face inches from mine, his eyes like two suns blinding me. I caught the scent of cloves in his clothing. The twin suns made me dizzy and detached from myself.

"Where is the other drive? You'll be okay. You want so badly to tell me. Just let it out and be at peace."

My will was weakened to a mere thread pulled too tight.

It broke.

"It's at my friend's house. Matt Rosen. Bond Street."

He was right. I felt unburdened and at peace.

"You will lead us there."

Completely pliant, I merely nodded and allowed them to take me back to their SUV.

MY PHONE HADN'T BEEN TAKEN from me, but it didn't matter. My brain was too soggy to remember how to use it and warn Matt. It was all I could do to pray that he would not be harmed.

We rolled down the street that was near Jellyfish Beach's tiny downtown and the Intracoastal Waterway. There were historic bungalows built for seasonal visitors in the 1920s, small apartment buildings from the 1950s, and a couple of new, flashy modernistic homes that didn't fit in.

Matt's pickup was in his driveway, and lights were on inside. I wished I could alert him, not just for his safety, but to protect the copy of the drive. Though I was mesmerized, I still felt anxious that all the work that we'd done would go to waste if this drive was found and destroyed.

Garth turned to me. "You will ring his doorbell and tell him we are your friends."

"I don't think she would be friends with us," the short one said. "Tell him we're your cousins from New Jersey."

"You will tell him we are your cousins, Garth and Bobby, from Bayonne," Garth commanded in his sing-song tone.

"And Bobby is your favorite."

"Ignore him. Come now, human, go to the door."

Garth opened my door. It seemed impossible to figure out how I could get myself out of the car until he yanked my arm and pulled me out. I walked robotically to Matt's tiny front porch, the two vampires close behind me. Moths fluttering around the light above the door distracted me.

"Knock," Garth said.

I knocked on the screen door's wooden frame.

"I will mesmerize him, because I am better at it," Garth whispered to Bobby. "You take over the woman."

"Who says you're better?"

"You know I am."

When Matt opened the door, his smile at seeing me quickly faded at the sight of the vampire thugs standing behind me. My spaced-out expression probably didn't help our feigned act of normalcy.

"Hi, Matt," I said in a flat voice. "These are my cousins from New Jersey."

"I didn't know you had cousins from New Jersey, but I can understand why you'd keep it secret."

"Hello, human friend of Missy," Garth said. "You will happily invite us into your home."

At that moment, it was as if my head popped up from under the water. Garth had released my mind from his control as he focused on mesmerizing Matt.

"Missy," Bobby said. I felt his consciousness probing mine.

I acted quickly and cast a warding spell to protect my mind from exterior forces before Bobby could mesmerize me.

"Tell your friend that I am your favorite cousin," Bobby said with the same tone Garth was using on Matt.

But it had no effect on me. The warding spell was working.

"Come in," Matt said in a dreamy voice as his face went slack.

I yanked the screen door open, pushed Matt out of the way, and slammed the front door shut in Garth's face, simultaneously constructing a protection spell.

A fist burst through the wood of the door. I jumped in fear

but didn't break my concentration. A cry of pain came from outside, and the fist withdrew.

The protection bubble was solidifying.

"Man, what is going on with those vampires?" Matt asked, rubbing his eyes groggily. "Is that why you texted me to be vigilant?"

"The tall one was beginning to mesmerize you, so you'd give him the backup drive. He already had me under his control, making me give up the original and reveal that a copy was here."

"How did they know you had it?"

"Agnes knew and told the others on the committee before I had the chance to tell her that I'd learned Beatrice was the one being blackmailed. I should have emailed the evidence to Agnes, but these vampire thugs showed up at my house and made me go to Squid Tower with the evidence. When they hauled me in front of their Policing Committee, I confronted Beatrice about it, and now she's fighting back."

"You need to email Agnes right away. We'll use my computer to extract the videos and other evidence you need. Can those two vampires get in here?"

"My protection spell should keep them out. Emphasis on 'should.' Never underestimate a vampire."

Sure enough, I sensed a shock as bodies collided with the protection bubble: two angry vampires using brute force to try to break through the barrier.

Meanwhile, Matt had connected the backup drive to his laptop on the desk in his bedroom. I stood behind him and guided him through the myriad files and folders to the specific items that were the most damning.

I'd never been in Matt's bedroom before, save to access the bungalow's one bathroom. He kept the place spotless, but the furniture was as old as the structure and had the musty smell of age. There was also the warm scent of Matt, the soap he had recently used, and the saltwater that must have dripped off him before he showered.

Another collision against the bubble startled me back to the problem at hand.

"These files are big," Matt said. "Each one will have to be attached to its own email. I'll send them to you, so you'll have your own copies and can forward them to Agnes from your email address to avoid confusion."

It took painfully long for them to download onto my phone before I could send them to Agnes.

"Done," I said.

"No, we're not done. We still have two vampires trying to get into my house."

"Let me see if Agnes can help." I called her, grateful that my abductors had been so confident in Garth's mesmerizing ability that they didn't think to confiscate my phone.

"Missy, I'll have to call you back," Agnes said. "I'm playing horseshoes at the moment."

"No, no, no. This is an emergency." I explained the situation, then said, "You need to make Beatrice call off the security guards."

"She's never been one to follow my commands, even though I'm the nest mother. Let me call Rudy, the owner of the security company. He'll call them off under threat of termination."

"And check your email," I urged. "I sent you the evidence."

Put aside, for a moment, the retired immortal creatures who have saved millions of dollars and invested them with the likes of Hugh Humbert to make them last for eternity.

What about working-class folks who were turned? They needed to continue working to pay the rent. Hopefully, after several decades, or a century or two, they'd save enough to allow them to retire. Until then, they must make a living, even though they were technically not living. And it's not easy to find a job when you can't come out during the daylight hours.

As I expected, the attacks against my protection ended. Rudy must have told them to leave or get fired.

So now, it was Agnes and I—possibly Schwartz and the others—against Beatrice.

No, scratch Schwartz. I didn't trust him.

CHAPTER 24

1N PERIL

After the thugs' SUV finally left, and we were certain they were gone for good, Matt invited me to stay for the rest of the night.

When he offered me his bed, with him sleeping on the couch, I declined. I was too strung out on adrenaline and would rather be in my bed with my cats.

I must be getting old. And why was Matt such a prude to sleep on the couch?

On my way home, I got a call from Detective Shortle.

"I thought you would want to know that I spoke with Monique Tibodet," she said. "It turns out she has a security camera in her backyard. There's video of a group of men abducting Tibodet's brother from a shed. Why he was in there, she wouldn't say, but we did identify Timothy Tissy and other individuals—including Matt Rosen. I need to speak to Rosen about this. He's not answering his phone."

"I'll make sure he calls you. Is this enough to bring charges against Tissy?"

"I believe so. But it will be hard to convict him without testimony from Carl Tibodet. His sister wouldn't let me speak with him."

No, you don't want him in a courtroom.

"Hopefully, Carl will come around," I said before we ended the call.

And hopefully, Lord Arseton would be too wrapped up in his legal problems to bother me.

Once home, it was hours before I finally drifted off to sleep.

Just before dawn, my phone woke me with an incoming text. Bleary-eyed, I saw it was from Agnes:

HELP ME

ᴀᴘᴏᴏᴏᴏᴘᴏ

AGNES MUST HAVE SEEN the evidence I emailed, along with my concise explanations. She must have been foolish and confronted Beatrice.

And now, she was in trouble. Maybe Beatrice had staked her already. If Beatrice could take down the oldest, most powerful vampire in the community, what could I possibly do about it? I was a witch, yes, but only a human.

A human who loved Agnes and had to do whatever I could to save her.

Should I bring Matt for backup? No, I'd already put him through too much. Few guys would be buried up to their neck beside a gator-infested river because of you and still have an affection for you afterward.

Angela? I wished I could invite her, but this mission didn't involve the Friends of Cryptids. I didn't know her well enough to ask her to risk her life in an internal vampire conflict.

I LOADED a tote bag full of charms, amulets, candles, and just about anything else I could think of. Electricians drive a van full of parts and materials they might need; that's what I was doing. I was a witch making a service call, not entirely certain about the challenge I was about to face.

I had enough gear and supplies to take on an army. But the truth was, one does not go toe-to-toe with an old, powerful vampire and expect to come out alive.

More than my magic, my secret weapon was daylight. I drove to Squid Tower shortly after sunrise, hoping to search for Agnes unmolested while all the vampires were asleep, or at least holed up in their condos with blinds closed.

The sun was still low in the sky when I crossed the drawbridge from the mainland. Gaps between beachfront homes and condo towers afforded views of a glass-smooth, cerulean ocean. The sun's reflection was like an arrow pointing toward the breakers. Normally, the view would cheer me up, but not today.

I didn't recognize the human guard at the gatehouse because I almost never came here during the day. He glanced at my vendor pass and opened the gate for me.

It was so strange to see the grounds of Squid Tower in full daylight. It looked like any of the other condo communities along the beach: lush landscaping, pastel-colored walls, shimmering blue pool, and asphalt parking lot. But it was all devoid of residents.

I parked and carried my tote bag into the lobby. My priority was to find Agnes and free her if she was being held captive. I prayed Beatrice hadn't murdered her. Neutralizing Beatrice was also crucial.

I went into the card room. The vampires say it has a splendid view of the ocean. Only I could see how beautiful it looked in the sunshine.

With the room to myself, I used a space in the corner to draw a magic circle with a dry-erase marker on the laminate flooring. Today, I would not cut any corners in the rituals. I wanted my spells to be as strong as possible.

First, I cast a protection spell to surround my body, followed by a warding spell to protect my mind from vampires who might try to mesmerize me. Needless to say, I already had two vampire-repellant amulets hanging from my neck.

I looked in the condominium office. I had a wild hope that the case that held all the units' keys would be unlocked, and I could take the ones I needed. But it wasn't, of course.

Then I remembered Beatrice had a key that opened this case. I realized this was how she got into Humbert's condo, allowing her to catch him off guard and stake him in his bed.

Wearing my magic armor, I headed upstairs. After the elevator took me to Agnes's floor, I prepared a spell to unlock her door. Unlocking doors was always a struggle for me. The complexities of a mechanical lock were harder to manipulate with magic than, say, an electronic lock.

I knelt before the door and built the spell. It was a terribly vulnerable place to be. Even though it was daytime, a sleepless vampire could come out into the hallway at any moment since there weren't any windows here. But I had no choice but to concentrate on the spell, sending my magic into the hardware, until I heard the telltale clicks of the deadbolt and the handle's lock.

Opening the door cautiously, I peered inside. A lamp was on in the living room, but no one was home. The sliding-glass doors at the end that faced the ocean were covered with thick burgundy drapes.

I searched the condo room by room, but was disappointed. An overturned chair in the bedroom suggested Agnes had been taken from here.

A pair of reading glasses sat on the side table next to the toppled chair. Agnes's energy clung to them. I performed the locator spell I had used earlier to find Matt. Everything seemed to go smoothly until the orb left the condo through a window. Instead of finding Agnes in a different condo or a public room, the orb shot up the height of the building and ended up hovering above the roof.

What did that mean? Agnes was in the building some-where, but her own energy couldn't find her?

Did that mean she had been destroyed, and the energy that remained from her was too faint for the orb to find?

My heart skipped a beat at that thought.

The next option was to look for Beatrice. I hoped I could break into her condo and find her sleeping, throw open the drapes or pull up the blinds, and sun-scorch her.

Yeah, I know. Sounds too easy.

I decided, instead, to break into the condo where Courtney was being held and free her. If Agnes was gone, and I was killed, too, Beatrice would have Courtney executed to cover up her own crimes. I needed to free Courtney now while I could.

CHAPTER 25

BEFORE THE SUN GOES DOWN

I was on my knees again in the hallway, this time in front of the vacant condo where Courtney was being held. There was no guard by the door today, probably because it was daytime, and the Policing Committee was confident Courtney wouldn't escape. A faulty assumption on their part.

The locks were just like Agnes's, but a second deadbolt had been installed. This one took several minutes for me to unlock with my spell.

Courtney was once again crouching on top of the armoire.

"Did I wake you?" I asked.

"You were making quite a racket with the locks."

"Sorry about that."

"You haven't been here for a while," she said.

"Nice to see you, too. You know, I'm not an attorney. You don't have a legal right for me to visit you under vampire law. I'm here today because I broke in."

She jumped to the floor, clearly curious.

"I'm setting you free if you help me rescue Agnes and capture Beatrice."

"Oh, I'll be happy to capture that nasty shrew. What happened?"

I told her about Agnes's cryptic text and the evidence I had found indicating Beatrice was the one who staked Humbert. I had no proof she murdered Heather, but it made sense, since Heather knew about Humbert's clients and, possibly, his blackmailing. Beatrice was aware I was interviewing her. It made sense that she would want to silence the young vampire.

"If we find Beatrice, how are we going to capture her?" Courtney asked.

"With a binding spell. Assuming it will work. Come on, let's go."

"How am I going to help you?" she asked, hesitant to leave the condo. "I can't go very far while the sun is up."

"You'll be my bodyguard. And for now, we'll stay inside, away from windows."

What I left out was that if we didn't find Agnes and Beatrice before nightfall, when the residents became active, things would get very dangerous.

Our first stop was Beatrice's condo. I performed my unlocking spell, realizing that it was rather noisy if you had vampire hearing.

Beatrice was old-school with her interior design. Most of the vampire homes I'd been in were decorated with human sensibilities. Some, like Agnes's, were stylish in a classic tradition. Mrs. Steinhauer constantly redecorated to stay at the forefront of fashion, while Schwartz's condo was mid-century modern—not because it was trendy, but because he had bought no furniture or accessories since the mid-twentieth century.

Beatrice's vision was pure Gothic. I mean, we're talking Transylvania Vampire Chic. She had stripped away the drywall, leaving bare concrete with sconces holding fake wooden torches. Chains hung from the ceiling. Heavy, medieval-style chairs faced an electric fireplace with a bearskin rug. An ancient portrait of a woman who looked like Beatrice in Renaissance-era attire hung above the fireplace.

I took a deep breath, prepared a binding spell nine-tenths of the way, then entered the master bedroom.

I stopped. Instead of a bed, there was a low oaken table with two caskets resting on top. His-and-Her coffins.

"That is so uncool," Courtney said. "I would never sleep in a coffin."

"It's such a cliché," I said.

Of course, the coffins were closed. Sure, why not make me extra scared?

In the movies, this was when you flung open the lids and drove stakes into the vampires, watching them writhe in agony before crumbling into dust.

I couldn't do that. This was a vampire couple's home in a community run under vampire law. Only the Policing Committee could rule that she be staked.

My only weapon against her was a binding spell, and a sleeping spell to keep her from struggling against her bindings. Unfortunately, I didn't know how well they would work on vampires.

"Open the lid with me," I told Courtney, as we stood by the

coffin with carved ornamentation that looked more feminine. Beatrice, I figured, would be the more dangerous of the two. If we were lucky, her husband would sleep through the whole thing.

"Hold her down while I cast my binding spell. Ready? One, two, three!"

We flung open the lid. The coffin was empty.

Courtney panted with fear. "Where did she go?"

I glanced behind me. "I hope she's not a sleepwalker."

"Do we have to open the other coffin?" Courtney asked. "Can't we let her husband sleep?"

"We need to make sure she's not in there. Come on—one, two, three!"

Flinging open the lid caused a draft of air to swirl the pile of dust around. There was nothing but dust, a man's pajamas, and a wooden stake.

"She staked her own husband?" Courtney asked.

"Yep. Maybe he learned about her affair."

Our job would have been so much easier if Beatrice had only been where she was supposed to be. Now we had to search this mausoleum of a condo tower to find her before the sun went down.

"Let's look for the duplicate keys for the condos Beatrice rents out," I said. "Beatrice is probably sleeping in the one where her lover lives."

"Such a black-hearted woman."

I studied Courtney's face. Her remarks made her sound like the newbie vampire she was. The undead keep most of their human personality and some of their values. But as time passes, many become more amoral and coldhearted. That is, if they were kind, decent humans before they were turned. Evil humans become beyond-evil vampires.

Beatrice's behavior was treacherous and cruel, besides violating the condo bylaws. But it wasn't so unusual for a vampire.

I found a keyring in a kitchen drawer. The kitchen, by the way, didn't look like it came from a vampire movie. But because it hadn't been updated since the building was constructed in the 1960s, it was pretty scary to me. Most vampires don't cook, so kitchen remodels aren't high on their priority lists.

The keyring had four keys, each labeled with the unit number. These were probably the keys Beatrice lent to contractors and handymen, including Humbert.

"We're going to break into all four condos?" Courtney asked.

"Only if Beatrice is in the last one we try. We'll go one by one and hope we're lucky."

And hope we don't get torn apart by any angry vampire renters we wake up.

"Good news," I said. "I see that one of these is the condo where you were detained. That means we only have to go to three."

First, we went to the vacant unit that I had searched for cameras. Beatrice was not there.

One unit was on the same floor as Beatrice's, just three doors down. I wished there was a way to do this without barging right in, but we had to catch Beatrice by surprise.

Once again, I prepared my binding spell almost to the point of casting it, like cocking a gun. Then, I unlocked the deadbolt and the doorknob.

We slipped inside quietly. The apartment was pitch black because of super-effective window coverings that kept out all sunlight. Faint cracks here and there allowed only minimal ambient light.

My eyes adjusted until I could barely see Courtney. Her nostrils flared, and she nodded, meaning she had picked up the scent of a vampire or two. We stood frozen while she listened with her heightened hearing.

Her head tilted like a confused dog's. She led the way to the second bedroom. I stayed right behind her, afraid of tripping over furniture.

The bedroom door was cracked. I pushed the door open.

There, in the darkness, sat Walt Whitman, reading from a piece of paper, whispering the words aloud.

"My lady's big butt, it drives me crazy, like I'm some nut, my eyes all hazy . . . Oh, hello. I didn't hear you two come in. I was just reading some modern American poetry."

"I believe that's called hip-hop," I said. "Sorry to intrude. I forgot you're one of Beatrice's renters. We let ourselves in with her duplicate key."

"No worries. But why?"

I hesitated. Could I trust Walt with the truth? A highly edited version would do.

"I believe she abducted Agnes and might murder her. If she hasn't already."

"Goodness gracious."

"And there are others she murdered. We need to find her and take her into custody. She's not in her condo, so we're assuming she's with her lover in the condo he rents from her."

"Which lover?" Walt asked.

"She has more than one?"

"Based on what I've observed living down the hall from her, yes. I don't know how her poor husband puts up with it."

"She took care of that problem," Courtney said.

"You mean . . . goodness gracious!"

"Do you know who these other lovers are?" I asked.

"I've seen and heard her with them in the hallway, but I'm too new here to know who they are."

"Well, let's go check out the other condo," I said to Courtney.

"I shall accompany you," said Walt. "You ladies need protection."

I wasn't sure how much protection he could offer, being seventy-two in body age and having suffered strokes when he was human. But a vampire with half strength was still better than a human.

"Thank you, Walt. You guys ready to head downstairs?"

The locks on 312 were smooth and, to my human ears, silent. Courtney and I went inside, with Walt waiting in reserve at the door.

Courtney sniffed the air. She nodded and held up a single index finger. Then, she pantomimed a gorilla.

Okay, only one vampire was here, and it was a man?

Loud, guttural snoring rang out from the master bedroom.

Yep, it was a man. Beatrice wasn't here.

The day was slipping by, and we still hadn't found her or Agnes.

I really didn't want to be searching for them after sundown.

CHAPTER 26

DANGEROUS WORDS

It was time to go back to my old tricks. I led my motley crew of vampires to Beatrice's Gothic crash pad to find a cherished object of hers. Yes, I was going to perform my locator spell again.

One thing that stood out in her condo's severe Transylvania-castle theme was an abundance of knitted objects. A pair of red knitted socks lay on the floor beneath her husband's coffin. Several brightly colored sweaters were stacked on an antique chest. A pink shawl was draped on one of the throne-like chairs in front of the electric fireplace.

Beatrice, the homicidal vampire, was an ardent knitter?

Finally, I found what I was looking for: a tote bag beside the chair, filled with yarn and a pair of knitting needles. The needles were alive with energy.

I asked my vampire friends to wait in the living room while I took the needles into the bedroom. There, I did a full-on spell-

243

casting production, complete with magic circle and lighted candles. I wanted this spell to be as effective as possible.

When the glowing orb appeared, I sent it in search of the source of Beatrice's energy, hoping she would be here at Squid Tower and not away at a knitting conference in Dubuque.

I waited in a semi-trance state, seeing the orb in my mind whizzing down hallways and up the exterior of the building, then down another hallway.

The orb slowed and stopped outside the door of 510.

No way. No, no, no. This condo belonged to Leonard Schwartz.

The orb passed through the door and made a beeline through the condo and into the master bedroom, where it found a sleeping Beatrice and was absorbed by her energy.

Before the orb dissolved, I saw a shiny bald head and a dome created under the sheet by Schwartz's pot belly.

I shuddered at the thought of the two of them together. Schwartz was long divorced, and thought of himself as a ladies' man, despite his loathsome appearance and personality. Beatrice was clearly emphasizing the "active" part of "active-adult community," especially with her husband out of the way. Now it made sense why Schwartz took her side on the Policing Committee and was so hostile toward Courtney.

To capture Beatrice right now would require binding Schwartz, as well. I couldn't afford to alienate him before he and the committee saw the evidence against his lover. It would be better to capture her later.

When I watched the orb being absorbed back into Beatrice, I tried to remember what had happened to the orb I had sent searching for Agnes. It had hovered futilely above the roof until

I lost patience and broke the spell. I never saw what happened to it—whether it remained up there or dissipated on its own.

I returned to Agnes's condo and found her reading glasses in the kitchen where I had left them. I had taken most of her energy from them in my spell, and only a trace remained. It wasn't enough to create a new orb, but I cast the spell anyway, hoping to reconnect with the original one.

Surprisingly, I did. The orb was still there, floating above the roof near the stairwell entrance and air-conditioning equipment.

The orb should have dissipated. Instead, it maintained itself, almost like a dog waiting for its master to come outside.

If Agnes had been in a penthouse condo, in the stairwell, or anywhere, the orb would have passed through the manmade materials to rejoin her.

In her bedroom closet, I found a pair of shoes she frequently wore. The shoes held more energy than the glasses had. I tried the spell again, hoping a more powerful orb would find her.

After the orb appeared, and my mind connected with it, it streaked straight through Agnes's window and shot two stories up to the top of the building. It stopped near the other, smaller, orb and hovered, bobbing as if in frustration.

This was puzzling. I went to the window the orb had passed through and opened the thick purple drapes. Agnes had a large three-bedroom end unit, meaning she had windows to the east and west, but also this one that faced north. A glance outside told me it was sunset.

Wait, didn't Agnes keep her hurricane shutters up year-round for sun protection? I went to the east- and west-facing windows and pushed the drapes aside to see the shutters blocking the view. Yes, the rising and setting sun would be punishing, but the north side would not be so bad.

The orb had exited this north window, passing through fabric and glass only—not the aluminum shutters.

Did orbs have difficulty passing through aluminum? I'd never noticed before when using this spell, because the orbs always managed to pass through walls or windows somehow.

But not at the top of Squid Tower.

Courtney and Walt were waiting for me in the hallway. I glanced at my watch.

"I think it's safe to go outside now," I said, explaining the results of my locator spell. "Let's go to the roof. I think Agnes is up there after all."

It was dark enough for the vampires to follow me from the stairwell out onto the roof. Agnes wasn't at the top of the stairs behind the metal fire door, as I had hoped. The two orbs were hovering nearby because my spell was still active, visible only to me.

They were above aluminum ductwork stemming from enormous air-conditioning condensers.

Now that I was near, the spell allowed me to sense the energy flowing from the orbs and conducting along the aluminum.

But not passing through it.

I studied the network of large ducts. Something odd caught my eyes. One duct turned at a right angle, but the elbow piece had been removed. One section was now open at its end and pumped cool air into the night. The end of the other duct was covered by a sheet of aluminum attached with duct tape.

I tore away the cover and peered into the opening. Agnes lay inside the duct, bound by steel cables too strong for a vampire to break, silenced by a gag.

I easily pulled her diminutive body from the duct and placed her gently on the roof.

Agnes looked at me in desperation while I untied her gag. She gasped when it came off.

"What is Beatrice planning to do with you? Why didn't she murder you right away?" I asked.

"She was going to announce tonight that I was Humbert's murderer. Then, she would oversee my execution."

"She didn't like you knowing she was the murderer."

"No, she didn't. Can you get these off me?"

"I'll free you as quickly as I can," I said, looking at the padlocks that held the cables together. They were simple security cables for securing heavy equipment. "I'm a little slow with my unlocking spell."

I broke the locator spell and focused on the padlocks. They were simpler than deadbolts.

One lock snapped open, followed by the second. She rubbed her sore wrists and ankles.

"Is Schwartz in on her scheme?" I asked.

"I don't think so."

"Did you know they're lovers?"

"Ye gods! What a horrible thought. Now I can't get the image out of my mind."

I didn't want to anger her, but I had to ask, "How did Beatrice capture you?"

"I believe she stole the spare key to my condo from the office downstairs. Those two brutes from the security service burst into my bedroom and took me before I could react. They are significantly younger in body age, and they carried spears to be used as stakes."

"No one seemed to mind when they forced me from my house and took the cameras and hard drives."

"If we get through this, I will have them fired."

"*If* we get through this?"

"Beatrice will come for me when she discovers I've been freed."

"There are four of us," I said.

She looked at me like I was an idiot before I realized that out of the four of us, one was a human and two were vampires of advanced body age. Beatrice, the two thugs, and any other vampires on her side would make short work of us, especially if they were armed.

"Don't forget about my magic," I said. "Let me cast a protection spell around us, and we'll go downstairs to a public area—"

The door to the stairwell opened with a loud metallic clang. Garth, Bobby, and Beatrice raced toward us so quickly, I didn't even see them knock the vampires of my team off their feet. Courtney fought Beatrice in midair, such a flurry of motion that I couldn't tell who was winning. It ended with Courtney, Agnes, and Walt prone on the roof, with Beatrice and her thugs holding spear tips against their chests.

I uttered the first two words of my sleep spell before Beatrice seized my throat and held me dangling in the air.

"You will not cast any spells, witch," she said, mesmerizing me with far more power and skill than the younger thugs had.

Game over.

"I call an emergency session of the Policing Committee," Beatrice said. "A quorum is unnecessary for an emergency session. Our current chairwoman is accused of the capital crime of destroying three of your fellow vampires—Humbert, his assistant, and my beloved husband. In the shared interest of our community, I sentence you to death by staking, Agnes Geberich, along with your accomplices Courtney Peppers and Walt Whitman."

"Accomplices?" Courtney sneered. "You mean witnesses to your crimes?"

"Witness," Walt said in a sonorous voice. "I have no mockings or arguments. I witness and wait."

"What are you talking about?" Beatrice asked.

"I believe in you my soul, the other I am must not abase itself to you."

Beatrice appeared baffled.

Walt went on and on, line after line, verse after verse, for the rest of "Song of Myself." I couldn't understand why he would choose this moment for a poetry reading.

Our foes didn't, either. They were confused by the silly old vampire who didn't realize his impending destruction.

Then, they were yawning, their eyelids were drooping, and their arms slackened. Beatrice's grip loosened, and I landed on my feet. My strength was fine, but my mind was still muddled.

When Bobby dropped his spear, Beatrice mustered the strength to bark an order.

"Kill the poet! His poetry is dangerous."

Her next sound was a snore. Beatrice and her two thugs dropped to the floor and curled up into comfy positions, happily sound asleep.

"Okay, Walt, that's enough," Agnes said.

"The poem has more parts."

"We're not going to survive if you put us to sleep, too."

"It's not as if I were boring them," Walt protested. "I overwhelmed their senses. I suspected that would happen and hoped it would save us."

"Well, you were boring *me*," Courtney said.

"The young today have such short attention spans."

I wanted to defend Walt Whitman's genius, but my mind was still foggy. How did this guy become one of the most famous American poets if he put everyone to sleep?

"Walt, did you hypnotize them?" I asked in a dreamy voice.

Agnes snapped her fingers in front of my face.

"Missy, you are no longer mesmerized. Put a binding spell on them," Agnes commanded. "Courtney, use those steel cables that were on me to lock the three of them together. I'm going downstairs to round up every able-bodied vampire I can find to help us move them into the condo where Courtney was held."

CHAPTER 27

THE POWER OF POETRY

"I dismounted my steed and rushed to the portico where Lady Bellamy had fainted in a heap. I crouched beside her and pulled her head to my chest," Martin read in his soft but matter-of-fact voice. "Her eyes fluttered open, and I kissed each one. I vowed to her I would never leave her again."

It was a typical night with the creative-writing group. Martin put down his tablet with a smirk. Regency romances were easy for him to write. They required no research because he had been alive as a human in the early 1800s. What he didn't realize was authenticity wasn't all it took to make a good story. And I would not be the one to tell him.

"Your romance stories are kind of boring," Gladys said.

"My stories are clean historical romance. Yours," Martin said, "are pornography."

"They are not. They are spicy."

The undead existence of Squid Tower residents had gotten

back to normal now that Beatrice was locked up and bragging about her crimes to any guard willing to listen.

Martin didn't share his work often. Unlike the few other men in the group, he didn't write adventure tales full of weapons and vehicles. After reading their stories, the men loved to argue about technical details.

The women in the group mostly stuck to romance stories and cozy mysteries. Occasionally, I would hear autobiographical tales with touches of literary insight.

The exception to our group, of course, was Walt Whitman. He read his famous poetry, including newer works the vampire wrote after his life as a human had ended and his body had allegedly been buried. Although we all knew who he was, Walt continued to insist his name was Wade Winkle.

"Is it Walt's turn?" Marjorie asked. "I want to hear him read. I love his voice."

"Me, too," said Doris. "It's dreamy. Your poetry transports me, Walt."

"It's Wade. But thank you. You're so kind. Do you mind if I begin?" he asked me.

He pulled a small leather-bound notebook from the pocket of the nineteenth-century jacket he wore, despite the Florida weather. He claimed the air-conditioning was too cold in the common rooms of Squid Tower.

He thumbed through the yellowed pages of his notebook. "This is an older work. Is that acceptable?"

"Of course," I said.

"This is called, 'I Hear America Singing.'"

He read, with a rich, sonorous voice, the verses I had struggled through in high-school English class. I once heard an audio recording of Whitman reading his poetry from late in his life. It was the same voice, but the old recording was tinny and scratchy, his voice sounding thin and feeble compared to tonight. Being a vampire definitely benefited Walt's poetry-reading performance.

Unlike when I had read the text of this poem, hearing it was so much more impactful. His emotion moved me, his diction hypnotized me, his metaphors sent my imagination soaring.

Next, he read "O Captain! My Captain!" By now, he was surpassing the time normally allotted for each member of the group. But no one seemed to care. Everyone wore a wistful smile, and many had their eyes closed as Walt's words transported them.

As he read, Walt didn't get tired or lose his voice. Instead, he seemed to draw strength from our enjoyment. His volume and timbre went up a notch, as did his enthusiasm.

As for me, well, as much as I was enjoying the reading, I was getting tired. I was close to nodding off. I didn't want to offend Walt, so I struggled to keep my eyes open and my head from dropping to my chest. This is what you get, I thought, for working daylight human hours and mixing them with vampire hours.

Yet, the vampires of our group were falling asleep, too. And this was way before their bedtime. Or, should I say, coffin-time?

I used my inner energies to steel my mind and avoid becoming affected like I had on the roof last night.

A snore came from my right. Sol's bald head with its pointy ears was tilted back, mouth open, eyes closed. His fangs were thankfully retracted, but he wasn't an attractive sight. A paper document slipped to the floor to my left. Gladys was slumped in her chair, completely asleep.

Walt was oblivious to the fact he was losing his audience. He continued reading, even more enthusiastically.

Another snore rang out, this time from Doris. Her mouth was open, with her fangs fully extended. My basic animal instinct made me want to flee.

Now, Walt's free verse was punctuated by a chorus of vampire snores. I was embarrassed by my writing group's behavior, but they clearly couldn't help it.

Walt finally noticed that his entire audience, save the solitary human, was asleep.

"Goodness gracious. I seem to have read for too long. I did not intend to overwhelm their senses."

"Don't take it personally. We all love your poetry," I assured him. "I think our group was a little too busy tonight with their pickleball and shuffleboard, trivia contests and art classes. They're just tuckered out."

"Well, I hope they enjoyed my reading. I most assuredly did."

This was too much of a coincidence. He saved us during Agnes's rescue by putting Beatrice and the two thugs to sleep. He clearly had a potent, almost magical ability to knock vampires out with his poetry. Perhaps, his "overwhelming their senses" was more than hypnosis.

He smiled and bid me good night. When he walked out of the room, I felt compelled to see where he went. He went down the hallway, out the back door, and across the pool deck. I followed him down the dune crossover and watched while he disrobed and jumped into the ocean naked. He swam parallel to the shore, up and down the beach, with strong, energetic strokes like a younger version of himself.

Did he get so much energy simply from reading to an audience?

When I returned to the community room, my writing group was still in dreamland. What kinds of dreams do vampires have? I didn't want to know.

However, I was convinced that my entire group had not passed out naturally. Clearly, Walt's poetry had put them to sleep, but it couldn't have been because of their boredom. They were enthralled by his performance at the beginning, savoring every word. They didn't fidget, check their phones, or exhibit any signs of boredom.

They were swept away by his poetry, and then swept to dreamland.

All the while, Walt's performance had grown increasingly energetic.

The obvious finally struck me: Walt was the cause of the acute enervation spreading through the community—the "vampire flu." He was exhausting the vampires of Squid Tower with his free verse.

Walt Whitman was a psychic vampire.

Yeah, sometimes I can be slow on the uptake. I simply never could have imagined that a vampire would be the supernatural creature I'd been searching for. He was, essentially, a different species of vampire.

Over the next nights, I showed up at Squid Tower even when I didn't have a home-health appointment. It was so I could surveil Walt and learn more about his soporific effects.

Of course, I couldn't see what he was up to inside his

condo, but I discreetly followed him whenever I spotted him out and about.

Walt apparently didn't have a car or didn't know how to drive. He took taxis to go on errands but did so only rarely. He spent most of his time, when not in his condo, reading books on the moon deck, swimming naked in the pool or ocean, and going on long walks on the beach.

He mingled with other residents from time to time, but his main interaction with his neighbors was giving impromptu poetry readings, such as reading by a beach bonfire like I had witnessed before. Sometimes, he read from his chaise lounge by the pool. Once, he read to a group of residents playing horseshoes.

And every single time he gave a reading, he left his audience asleep, or so sluggish they could barely move.

After every reading, he walked away with an extra spring in his step.

It was only logical to conclude that Walt wasn't simply putting his audiences to sleep. He was taking energy away from them.

As a witch, I knew a lot about energy—that which we have inside of us and that which we harvest from the elements. People like me, born with the magic gene, can generate more internal energy than a normal person. But our energy can be depleted. Using it for magic sucks it from our bodies and spirits, leaving us exhausted and needing to replenish it.

That was what was happening to the vampires, except they weren't using up their energy; it was being taken from them.

"Have you ever heard of this phenomenon?" I asked Luisa at the botanica after telling her the entire story.

"No, but—"

The bells above the door tinkled. Mrs. Lupis and Mr. Lopez strolled inside in their gray suits.

"We got your message," Mr. Lopez said. "You found the mysterious creature."

"A psychic vampire," Mrs. Lupis said, like a proud parent. "We've seen evidence that they exist, but we've never found one."

"We've searched unsuccessfully for years," Mr. Lopez said. "We are certain this psychic vampire is the unknown supernatural creature you traced to Squid Tower."

"So am I."

"I've never heard of this kind of vampire," Luisa said.

"Just like normal vampires sustain themselves with blood, psychic vampires feed upon their victims' psychic energy," Mrs. Lupis explained.

"This psychic vampire has been feeding on other vampires rather than humans. Is that normal?" I asked.

"We don't know. This species is a mystery to us. There have been cases when, in times of famine, vampires have harvested blood from other vampires. So, I would not be surprised if psychic vampires also preyed upon vampires."

"I guess vampires are rich in psychic energy, given their supernatural powers," I said. "You would think, though, that psychic vampires would more commonly feed on humans because of our abundance and gullibility."

I thought about Walt's method of predation: captive audiences giving him all their attention.

"Do psychic vampires feed *only* on psychic energy?" I asked. "Or do they drink blood, too?"

Mr. Lopez shrugged. "We don't know."

I didn't recall ever seeing Walt with his fangs extended. Did he even have fangs?

"We would like to interview this vampire," Mrs. Lupis said, "to enter relevant information into our database of monsters."

"Preferably here, rather than Squid Tower," Mr. Lopez said squeamishly.

"I could invite him," I said. "I can't guarantee he'll come."

"What is his name?" Mrs. Lupis asked as she pulled out a notepad.

"Walt Whitman."

They both looked at me in shock.

"Yep, the poet. He was turned very late in life. If there's a body in his grave, it's not his."

"How could his poetry drain people of their psychic energy?" Luisa asked. "His work was breakthrough, and it inspires me to this day."

"It's not the poetry that's draining his victims. It's his vampiric powers," Mrs. Lupis explained. "He could read the dictionary, and it would have the same effect."

I didn't want to admit it, but Walt Whitman had put me to sleep on many occasions in school, and the vampire poet himself had been nowhere near me.

THAT EVENING, I found Walt skinny-dipping in the pool, causing the water-aerobics class to flee.

258

"Oh, I'd prefer not to ride in a motorcar," he said. "Can't the biographers come speak to me here?"

I felt it a wise idea to obscure the true roles of the representatives of the Friends of Cryptids Society. I let Walt believe they were interested in his literary prowess. Next, I had to convince them to come to this "lurid nest of vampires," as Mr. Lopez had put it.

You would think, in their roles, they wouldn't be so squeamish about the monsters they researched. I supposed that was why they needed people like me.

Two nights later, I waited for them at the gate and directed them where to park their rental car. They got out, searching the darkness for hidden vampires.

"It's quiet now," I said. "But in an hour, watch out. It's Bingo Night."

I led them to the front entrance, handing each a cloth amulet attached to a leather cord.

"These have vampire-repellant magic. The vampires here are well-behaved, but you should wear them just in case."

My words did not have a calming effect on Mr. Lopez and Mrs. Lupis.

"So, where are you guys from?" I made a lame attempt at small talk as we walked. "You're always all business when you show up, then you immediately disappear. Your car looks like a rental. Do you fly here?"

"No," Mrs. Lupis said. "We're based in—"

"A large city in Florida," Mr. Lopez cut in.

"Okay. Is that where the Society is headquartered?"

"No. They're in a larger city elsewhere."

"I see."

The more time I spent with these guys, the more mysterious they seemed. I used to think of them as superior beings, but tonight, they seemed vulnerable.

I rather enjoyed it.

We passed through the ground floor of the building and exited at the pool deck. Walt had said he would be basking in the moonlight, but the pool area and moon deck were empty as the residents prepared for Bingo Night. I led my guests along the boardwalk to the beach. A solitary figure with a long beard stood chest-deep in the ocean. I hoped he wasn't naked.

We descended the stairs of the dune crossover and approached the water's edge.

"Mr. Walt Whitman, I'd like you to meet Mr. Lopez and Mrs. Lupis."

He'd agreed when I arranged this meeting to give up his pretense of calling himself Wade Winkle.

"Good evening, sir. We're here to—"

A wave receded, revealing that yes, Walt was naked.

Mr. Lopez couldn't finish his line, so Mrs. Lupis stepped in.

"We're here to speak to you about your supernatural abilities. We belong to a scholarly society that studies them."

"I thought you were literary biographers."

"They are, in a way," I improvised. "They believe your literary talent is so remarkable that it must be supernatural."

"I simply seek the truth and beauty in the human experience," he said. "Well, I did when I was human."

"Sir, can you tell us how you became a psychic vampire?" Mrs. Lupis asked.

"A what?"

"A psychic vampire is one that sustains himself with the psychic energy of others," I explained.

"Indeed? I thought I had simply come back from the dead and achieved immortality as a vampire, but with no need for anything to sustain myself at all. I'm living here with these other vampires who need blood."

"Walt, you don't need blood, but you need psychic energy," I said. "Do you ever wonder why everyone falls asleep during your poetry readings?"

"I thought it was because I was overwhelming their senses."

"Nope. You're sucking psychic energy from them." I was blunt, but he needed to know the truth.

"Oh. That is distressing."

"It doesn't mean they don't love your poetry. They're simply tapped out."

"Sir," Mr. Lopez, finally recovered from the shock of Walt's nudity, spoke up. "You didn't answer the question about how you became a vampire."

"Oh, it was Henry."

"Sorry?"

"I was bedridden with pneumonia for months, went to sleep, and didn't wake until I found myself in a pine casket. Quite a frightening way to wake up, I should say. I pushed open the lid and crawled out onto a table covered in flowers."

"Who was the last person you saw before you died?"

"Henry. He was reading me his poetry."

"Henry who?"

"My old pal, Henry Wadsworth Longfellow, of course."

"But Longfellow died years before you," Mrs. Lupis said.

261

Walt giggled. "That was supposed to be our little secret. He was dead, but he came back to visit and read to me."

"Could Longfellow be a psychic vampire?" I asked.

Walt thought for a moment. "I used to think his poetry was too beautiful; that's why it put me to sleep. But I suppose it killed me in the end, because hearing his verse was the last thing I remembered. After I died, though, he helped me begin a new life."

"How so?" Mr. Lopez asked.

"When I escaped from the coffin, he showed up at my house and told me I was a vampire, and it was time to move on to my afterlife. So, I moved to Florida."

For most of us, Florida is known as God's Waiting Room. For the undead, it's just another place to retire.

"Is Mr. Longfellow in Florida, too?" Mr. Lopez asked.

"Only during the winter."

Mr. Lopez and Mrs. Lupis nodded to each other while scribbling notes.

"Thank you for your time, sir," they said simultaneously.

"Walt, I would suggest cutting back on the number of readings you do here at Squid Tower. It's taking a toll on the residents. Why don't you do some readings at the public library?" I suggested. Angela would be furious at this suggestion. "Regular humans should be an excellent source of psychic energy."

"That is a splendid idea. Expose myself to a new audience."

The waves dipped down to his knees, exposing himself to us yet again.

CHAPTER 28

A MOTHER OF A PROBLEM

U nder Agnes's threat to cancel their contract, the security company fired Garth and Bobby. Furthermore, Agnes added to the contract a stipulation that individual residents or committees could no longer directly assign security personnel, as Beatrice had with the two thugs, unless the full board approved.

Beatrice was an open wound that must be dealt with. With her detained, and Schwartz forced to recuse himself, Agnes formed a new Policing Committee. They reviewed the evidence I provided and investigated further on their own.

The case against her was damning.

She even proudly admitted murdering Humbert, his assistant Heather, and her husband.

"We have no choice but to stake her," Agnes told me when I was there for a creative-writing class, a blood-red tear inching down her cheek. "She's been my friend for over a hundred years."

It wasn't my place to comment on vampire justice. All I could do was give her shoulder a comforting squeeze.

On the very night the Policing Committee sentenced Beatrice to be staked, she escaped. When Agnes and the new members arrived at the condo to announce her fate, she was gone.

She couldn't have escaped through the windows or from the balcony, because all the openings were sealed from the outside by hurricane shutters. The lock on the outside of the door to keep her in hadn't been tampered with.

The guard stationed outside the door said he had seen nothing. Of course, that's what you get when your justice system is run by amateurs. Peter Wonderment from Rochester, New York, was hardly a trained prison guard. He was a retired pharmacist who'd been turned in his seventies. He had no qualifications at all, except for eagerly volunteering for things.

Agnes believed Peter was mesmerized by the older and more powerful Beatrice and unlocked the door at her command.

Personally, I believed Schwartz also might have assisted Beatrice in her escape, but there was no way to prove it. They should have put a surveillance camera outside the door. Centuries-old vampires are rarely technophiles. Again, when a community has very little experience with crime, it has very little know-how to deal with it.

The Policing Committee and HOA officially banned Beatrice from Jellyfish Beach and its unincorporated territory. That's as far as their authority extended. If the murderer were caught trespassing, she would be staked. The long arm of the law seemed awfully short in this case.

Believe me, I had no blood lust to see Beatrice staked. Still, I felt unsatisfied that she had escaped with her only punishment being banishment. For now, however, that would have to do.

When Courtney's overdue payment finally arrived, I flashed it in front of Luisa's nose at the botanica.

"See, detective work can be a good alternate stream of revenue for us."

"You spent many more hours on it than you billed," she replied. "You were almost killed. Your boyfriend was almost killed."

"He's not my boyfriend, and that incident had nothing to do with the vampire murder investigation."

Luisa shrugged. "What you bring us are alternate streams of crazy."

The bells above the door tinkled, and Carl shuffled in.

"How are you feeling, Carl?" I asked.

He moaned.

"I think that was a happy moan."

He lurched down the second aisle and returned with a statuette of Papa Legba.

"Why does Madame Tibodet need another statuette of him?" I asked. "She must have tons of them."

"They break easily," Luisa said, chasing after Carl to note the price tag on the figurine's base. "Especially when zombies handle them."

Carl left the shop and got into a ride-share car.

"You'd think that woman would be more careful about sending her zombie brother on errands after what happened," Luisa said.

Before the bells had stopped tinkling after Carl's exit, Mr.

Lopez and Mrs. Lupis walked in wearing their ever-present gray suits.

"Greetings," Mrs. Lupis said to us. "We have another assignment for you."

Luisa caught my eye. She frowned and shook her head. I admit I'd been too distracted lately to be much help running the shop, but I couldn't say no to the Friends of Cryptids Society of the Americas. Not after all the money they invested in us.

"We're kind of busy," Luisa said.

"There have been reports of a new creature in Jellyfish Beach. The reports have been second-hand, and no one has identified the species."

"That's all you can tell us?" I asked.

"The sightings have been outside of town—in the wetlands, lakes, and beaches."

"And what are we supposed to do about it?" Luisa demanded.

"Keep your eyes and ears open. If the creature attacks anyone, you must track it down."

"Oh, my," I said.

"Wonderful," Luisa said.

"We'll see you later," Mrs. Lupis said.

Luisa and I looked at each other and rolled our eyes.

⸎

MEANWHILE, I had a monster of my own to deal with. She was a human witch, of the black-magic category. The Friends of

Cryptids didn't catalog humans who had the magic gene or other paranormal abilities. Maybe they should. An evil witch could cause as much harm as a rogue cryptid.

After having my second nightmare about my mother in recent months, I called Detective Shortle to ask her about the rituals at the houses of worship.

"After I spoke to you last, I shared your advice with all the denominations to dismantle and dispose of those weird shrines before anyone entered the building," she told me. "And by the way, no one has produced any security-camera footage of the vandals."

Because a cloak of invisibility must have been used to hide whoever was doing this. But I couldn't say that to Shortle.

"But something odd happened at the Catholic church on Sunday. When the first mass of the morning was going on, a parishioner arrived late. Her screams, just outside the main door, disrupted the service. When the ushers checked on her, they found she had no injuries but had suffered a mental-health issue."

"What had she seen?"

"She couldn't express anything coherent except the word 'monster.'"

This, of course, piqued my interest. Had this creature been about to set up the ritual tableau?

"Were any strange objects left at the door?"

"No. Nothing. Security footage showed her walking briskly to the door, stopping suddenly, and going into hysterics. This episode might be completely unrelated, but I wanted to mention it."

"I'm glad you did," I said. "I want to speak with this woman."

"I don't think I can violate her privacy like that. She was briefly hospitalized after the incident."

That meant privacy laws protected her.

"You can speak to her," I said. "You're a police detective, and she interrupted a crime in progress."

"What crime?"

"She saw something that traumatized her," I said. "You have a pretext to speak with her. And I can accompany you."

"Listen, Mindle, I've told you about these incidents because you're . . ."

"A kook?"

"No, I was going to say that you're knowledgeable about supernatural stuff. Vandalizing houses of worship could be the work of someone obsessed with that kind of nonsense."

"Look, it's only a matter of time before someone gets hurt. That woman was traumatized, and it could have been worse. Please help me speak to her."

"You were a nurse, not a psychologist."

"I think I can get the information I need. Don't you want the vandalism to stop?"

"Of course. There isn't much crime in Jellyfish Beach. Incidents like this get too much attention from the public."

Ah, so it was bad publicity that most bothered Shortle.

"Imagine how much good press you'll get if you solve it," I said.

"There have been cases in which the police used psychics to help solve disappearances. I've never heard of detectives working with botanica owners. Are you sure you're not a witch? You never gave me a straight answer."

"I like to keep my spiritual side private."

She nodded and frowned with concentration. "Okay."

"Okay, what?"

"I'll interview the woman in question, and you can come with me."

"Thank you. And don't worry, I'll behave."

I intended, however, to push the boundaries of good behavior.

To afford Meg Gretcherson privacy, we didn't go to her workplace, a marketing firm. Nor did we show up at her home. Instead, we invited her to the police department, where we met with her in a conference room. I was introduced as Shortle's "researcher."

"Ms. Gretcherson, can you describe what you saw at the church's entrance?" Shortle asked.

"All I can remember is someone scary-looking who was carrying bones. I guess my mind is trying to blank it out."

I asked, "Was it a woman in her late sixties with black hair and glasses with large frames?"

"No. It was a man."

"Are you certain?" Shortle asked.

"Yes."

Well, that ruled out my mother doing the deed herself, but the man could be her lackey.

"Can you describe the man?"

"No. Like I told you, my mind has blanked it out."

I had come prepared for a problem like this. It was called a recollection spell, and I confess I'd used it once on myself when taking the exam to renew my nursing license. I knew how to cast it without any obvious rituals. It simply took a lot of concentration while invoking the words under my breath. Shortle was paying too much attention to Ms. Gretcherson to notice my lips moving.

When the spell took effect, the subject's pupils dilated noticeably.

"He was tiny for a man," she blurted out. "Like a dwarf. No, like an imp. He was green and naked with horns and a corkscrew tail like a pig's."

Shortle glanced at me with a look of concern, but I kept my eyes on Ms. Gretcherson.

"In fact, I remember now: he grunted like a pig. The creature was so unnatural, so revolting. He had a bundle of human bones under one arm and carried a cloth sack in his other. I startled him when I ran up the steps and screamed. He dropped the bones. I remember the sound they made as they clattered down the stairs. He snorted and made a threatening gesture toward me. That's when I grew dizzy and knew I was going to faint. Just before I went out, there was something else. Something odd."

Shortle and I remained quiet, hoping she would go on.

"He spoke. Yes, now I remember he spoke in a human voice. He said, 'Sorry, Mistress Ophelia. I will complete the task another time.' Then, I passed out."

Shortle asked her a few more questions. But there was

nothing more to the story other than waking up with the male usher squatting beside her outside the church as he called 911. She was taken to the ER for tests and was released several hours later.

Shortle turned to me to see if I had any other questions.

"Thank you for your time, Ms. Gretcherson," I simply said.

I had no other questions because I had the answer I needed. Ophelia was my mother.

♈

I RECOUNTED this story to Luisa and Matt in the botanica.

"I was hoping I'd never have to deal with my mother again," I said. "Except, maybe we'd send each other birthday or Samhain cards. Possibly, we would even meet for lunch someday. I guess I was naïve. After my magic healed her kidney disease and she was stripped of her magical powers, she stopped trying to kill me. It didn't mean we'd be friends, but at least we'd stop being enemies. Or so I thought. But now it looks like she got her powers back, and I'm going to have to fight her again."

"No, you don't have to," Matt said. "This has nothing to do with you."

"She's working black magic in our town. Why, I don't know. But I need to stop her."

"You have plenty on your plate already," Luisa said. "Lots of shelves to stock. You have no time to fight evil sorceresses."

"Someone has to do it."

"There are other witches in Jellyfish Beach," Luisa said. "Angela, for instance."

"I can't dump this on her. It has nothing to do with the Friends of Cryptids Society. The problem here was created by my mother, so I bear the responsibility of fixing it."

"Why don't you just forget about it for now," Matt said. "There hasn't been any true harm yet."

"That we know about. And every week, worshippers are in danger of losing their souls."

Matt shrugged. "I'm hungry. You guys want to order—ow! What the heck?"

The were-crab had somehow leaped into the air and grabbed Matt's earlobe in its dominant claw. It dangled there, its other nine legs moving.

"The Devil Crab," Luisa said.

"It's a were-crab," I explained. "I guess being supernatural allows it to jump like that."

"Get it off me!"

"She's very crabby, being trapped in a crab's body."

"Why would anyone want to shift into a crab, of all things?" he asked. "Ow!"

The crab had swung around like a gymnast and seized his nose in her other claw.

"Don't hurt her!" I screamed and seized Matt's wrist before he snapped the crab's claws off.

"Don't they grow their claws back?" he asked.

"Well, stone crabs do. I don't know about blue land crabs."

"Can you please help me here?"

I cast a quick spell, and the were-crab's claws released. She dropped to the floor and scurried underneath a product shelf.

Matt gingerly touched his nose and earlobe. "Am I injured?"

"You're fine," I said.

"I'm ordering from the deli down the street, and I'm getting the crab salad," he announced. "Do you hear that, Devil Crab?"

"Let's all relax and count our blessings," Luisa said. "For the moment, this crab is the only monster we need to be concerned about. Let's enjoy the peace while we can."

"Amen," I said. Though I had doubts about how long the peace would last.

WHAT'S NEXT

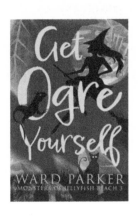

Book 3 of Monsters of Jellyfish Beach: *Get Ogre Yourself*

There's a new monster in town.

I'm so grateful Jellyfish Beach has preserved its small-town charm, despite the new residents who constantly arrive here. Especially when many of them aren't human.

Case in point: a species of ogre from Venezuela and Colombia called the munuane. Known as the "Grandfathers of Fishes," legend has it that these ogres don't take kindly to humans who over-fish or otherwise abuse the environment. So, when fishermen and hunters start turning up dead around town, my handlers from the Friends of Cryptids Society suspect a munuane is to blame.

Who is assigned to investigate? Yep, yours truly. With help from Matt, naturally, along with all the magic I can muster.

The police don't suspect a hairy ogre from South America. And their "usual suspects" are surely innocent in my eyes. But, like most of my life, the investigation gets weird.

And dangerous.

Then, wouldn't you know it, my black-magic sorceress mother has to turn up and make my life even more complicated.

Will evil prevail? Ogre my dead body!

Dive into a wacky world of murder, magic, and mayhem with the "Monsters of Jellyfish Beach." Get them at Amazon, Barnes & Noble (paperback only) or via wardparker.com

GET A FREE E-BOOK

Sign up for my newsletter, and get *A Ghostly Touch*, a Memory Guild novella, for free, offered exclusively to my newsletter subscribers. Darla reads the memories of a young woman, murdered in the 1890s, whose ghost begins haunting Darla, looking for justice. As a subscriber, you'll be the first to know about my new releases and lots of free book promotions. The newsletter is delivered only a couple of times a month. No spam at all, and you can unsubscribe at any time. Get your free book for all e-readers or as a .pdf at wardparker.com

ACKNOWLEDGMENTS

I wish to thank my loyal readers, who give me a reason to write more every day. I'm especially grateful to Sharee Steinberg and Shelley Holloway for all your editing and proofreading brilliance. To my A Team (you know who you are), thanks for reading and reviewing my ARCs, as well as providing good suggestions. And to my wife, Martha, thank you for your moral support, Beta reading, and awesome graphic design!

ABOUT THE AUTHOR

Ward is also the author of the Memory Guild midlife paranormal mystery thrillers, as well as the Freaky Florida series, set in the same world as Monsters of Jellyfish Beach, with Missy, Matt, Agnes, and many other familiar characters.

Ward lives in Florida with his wife, several cats, and a demon who wishes to remain anonymous.

Connect with him on social media: Twitter (@wardparker), Facebook (wardparkerauthor), BookBub, Goodreads, or check out his books at wardparker.com

PARANORMAL BOOKS BY WARD PARKER

Freaky Florida Humorous Paranormal Novels
Snowbirds of Prey
Invasive Species
Fate Is a Witch
Gnome Coming
Going Batty
Dirty Old Manatee
Gazillions of Reptilians
Hangry as Hell (novella)
Books 1-3 Box Set

The Memory Guild Midlife Paranormal Mystery Thrillers

A Magic Touch (also available in audio)

The Psychic Touch (also available in audio)

A Wicked Touch (also available in audio)

A Haunting Touch

The Wizard's Touch

A Witchy Touch

A Faerie's Touch

The Goddess's Touch

The Vampire's Touch

An Angel's Touch

A Ghostly Touch (novella)

Books 1-3 Box Set (also available in audio)

Monsters of Jellyfish Beach Paranormal Mystery Adventures

The Golden Ghouls

Fiends With Benefits

Get Ogre Yourself

My Funny Frankenstein